ISBN-13: 978-1-952412-20-2

Cover design: 100Covers.com
Published By: Vagabond Publishing
Printed in the United States of America

I0599103

Dark Deception

TABLE OF CONTENTS

1

"Get him alive if you can, but get him!"

The mob yelled out in anger and eagerness, ready to be released after their quarry.

"Search every ravine, every crevice. But the fiend must be found!"

More cries of agreement, the crowd's anger feeding off the words. Long torches were waving in the air as their voices yelled in cacophony.

"Are you ready? Then light your torches and go!"

The torches were set ablaze, and baying hounds strained at their leashes as they led the way. The mob poured through the village streets, women and children looking on in fear and horror as they passed.

"Oh, Jack, I feel so bad for him."

I looked away from the black and white film to glance down at the head of wavy red hair that was leaning against my chest. I squeezed her with the arm wrapped around her shoulder, pulling her tighter as I bent to kiss the top of her head. It was our third official date, and I still couldn't believe I could be so lucky.

"You feel bad for the monster, Karen? I think you're supposed to empathize with the people he hurt."

"But he doesn't know any better. No one bothered to tell him the difference between right or wrong, they just chained him up and then released him on the world." She twisted around to stare at me with serious green eyes. "Would you hunt down and kill some poor Nox who was raised that way?"

The conversation had turned more serious than I'd expected, so I took a moment to consider the question. My first impulse was to say no, but then I really put it in context with some of the things I've seen and done over the last ten years. "Yeah," I said hesitantly. "If they killed someone, I'd have to chase them down. I wouldn't kill them, though, unless they didn't give me a choice."

Karen looked deeply into my eyes for several seconds, biting on her lower lip in a way that drove me crazy. Finally, she nodded and turned back to the movie as she leaned against my chest again.

On the screen, we watched as Frankenstein's monster was chased into the old windmill. He tossed the doctor who gave him life from a high window, then was burned alive as the rampaging villagers set the building on fire with their torches.

As we watched the saccharine happy ending, I couldn't stop thinking about Karen's question. What if some of the Nox I'd hunted down and killed through the years really were just misunderstood, or nothing more than the product of a bad upbringing? Could they have been saved? Maybe someone with the right skills could have rehabilitated them, turned them into functioning members of society once more without the blood lusts or anger that drove them to break the centuries-old Covenants between Nox and humans.

When the credits started rolling, Karen stretched her arms up with a little moan that I'd come to recognize as a contented sound. She stretched out on my old couch, with her feet curled at the far end as she slid her head down to my lap so she could look up into my eyes again.

"I can hear those cogs turning, Jack." She smiled at me, reaching up with a red-nailed finger to stroke my cheek. "What are you thinking about?"

"You," I said with a grin. "Laying on my couch, in my house, on a date. How did I ever get so lucky?"

"I ask myself that question every day," she said, running her hand through my wild dark brown hair and pulling me down as she lifted up. Our lips met, and I felt the sparks shoot through my body that happened every time we kissed.

Karen and I had met only two months earlier, while I was working a case to find a kidnapped girl. She was a reporter with KRSA, one of San Antonio's big stations, and told me about a string of similar kidnappings across town over the previous three months. With her help, I'd managed to track down the lamia responsible, rescuing the kids before the deranged Nox could abduct a ninth child and then eat them to satisfy her ravenous hunger.

A month after that, there was a confrontation with the person who had killed my sister a decade ago. I'd long thought that her killer was already dead but discovered the truth when someone hired my bounty hunter friend Nyk to track down the person known as The Magpie. That confrontation had clued me in on the existence of an organization called the Circle.

It also made me realize how much Karen cared for me, when she heard the reports over her scanner and rushed to the warehouse district to make sure I was okay. A week later, while we shared lunch at Luigi's and discussed our work, I finally

3

worked up the nerve to ask her out on a date. She grinned, said it was about time, and told me to pick her up at the station the next evening after the five o'clock broadcast.

For the first date, she dragged me into a bowling alley. I hadn't bowled since high school, and back then I had never been very good at it. We had a blast, though, with Karen beating me in the first two games. I managed to score 192 in the third, however, winning by a single point. A victory that soothed my bruised ego and satisfied my ultra-competitive side.

On the second date, we went to a mini golf place on the north side of town. It was only a mile from the old apartment my sister and I had shared before she ran away to work for Billy Wish, and yet I had never known it was there. We had a night of fun and enjoyment as we whacked little red and blue balls around the short greens. I was so entranced with Karen that it didn't bother me at all when she beat me yet again.

Dinner and a movie at my place for the third date had been her suggestion. One I'd happily agreed to before remembering what a mess my little house was. After living there for nine years, I'd finally started working on all the necessary renovations I'd planned when I bought it, but I was barely started on the process. To be honest, I'd only managed to sand and refinish the floors in the living room and spare bedroom after a month of hard work. I like to think I'd have gotten more done without my job as an investigator taking up most of my time, but I knew better.

Inviting Karen into my very sparsely furnished home had been stressful, as I kept waiting for her to look around in disapproval and decide we weren't right for each other after all.

4

Instead, she exclaimed happily that it was a cozy little house. After dinner, she had settled onto the old couch comfortably, holding out her arms to invite me to join her before we started the movie.

When our kiss ended, she moaned happily and settled her head back onto my lap. "You are a good man, Jack Dahlish. I know that if you were faced with Frankenstein's monster, you would have tried to find out why he killed before you acted."

"Sometimes you don't have that luxury," I told her. "When people are dying, you have to act fast to prevent another death." The Filii Nox didn't have any kind of prison system, or any way to punish transgressors. If I thought a human prison could hold whatever creature I was after, I was more than happy to turn them over to my friend on the police force. If not, then I had to solve the problem in the only other way possible.

"Maybe not, but I think you put more thought into it than most other people would." She reached up to run a creamy pale finger over my chest. The talisman I always wore was under my shirt there, and she ran her nail around the edges of the coin that hung on a thin silver chain. "Do you think the others who wear one of the Nine would pause to consider *why* a Nox broke the Covenants?"

That made me silent with thought for a few moments. In the ten years since I'd come into possession of the talisman, I'd only met one of the other holders. And that was a very brief meeting, as he passed through town on the trail of a dangerous creature. I'd offered to help in the search, but he'd only laughed and said I wasn't ready for that. I had no idea what the rest of the Nine were like. We were called that for the simple reason that nine of the coins existed in the world, talismans that gave us the ability to detect Nox through their human disguises and track them through essences that could linger for days or months, depending on the strength of the creature.

"Never mind," Karen said with a low laugh. A smile was quirking her lips as she watched my face while I was deep in thought. "What's next for movie night?"

Shaking my head to release the thoughts of my talisman and the Nine, I reached over to the small table beside the couch for the remote. Backing out of the now black screen, I scrolled through the menu to the next movie I'd selected for our date. It might have been a little hokey, but Karen seemed to be enjoying the old creature features of the '30s so far.

"Bela Lugosi as Dracula," I said, pressing the button to start the movie. "It's not even close to the reality of vampires, but I've loved this movie since I was a kid. My dad and I used to watch it all the time."

Karen rolled onto her side, snuggling closer to me as the movie began. I stared down at her as she became entranced by the opening scenes, marveling once again at how lucky I was to be there with such a beautiful woman.

There was something about Karen that had drawn me to her from the first moment we met. Even when I'd wanted nothing more than to avoid any kind of attention from the press, I hadn't been able to resist continuing to meet with her and discuss the case of the missing kids. I'd even opened up to her about the supernatural world on that first day, telling her about the Filii Nox, creatures created by the gods many millennia ago. I'd told her about the amulet I wore, and the powers it provided that made me a kind of policeman of the supernatural world. It gave me the abilities to protect humanity from Nox that went rogue, and sometimes to protect Nox themselves from threats to their communities.

I still couldn't explain why I had been so willing to tell her so much. It was knowledge that very few people had, and yet I'd spilled it to her not even twelve hours after we met. But I continued to feel that same desire to tell her anything. When I was working a case, we'd talk about it over lunch or while she was being prepped for her newscasts every night. I had to moderate the things I said when other people were around, of course.

Whatever the reason, it felt good to have someone to talk with so openly. To have a woman to talk with. A girlfriend to share my worries and concerns with. I felt her hand moving, searching for and then wrapping around mine as she watched the movie. In that moment, the world could have been crumbling around us and it wouldn't have diminished my intense happiness.

2

I was still deliriously happy when I woke the next morning. As I stretched contentedly, I thought back to the long kiss we'd shared standing beside Karen's car in the cold night. Karen and I were both shivering by the time it ended, and I'd stood there with my hands buried in my pockets as I watched her drive away and turn off my street at the stop sign.

Despite the late night, I felt rested and refreshed as I looked at my phone and saw it was still fifteen minutes before my normal alarm went off. I swiped the screen and turned off the alarm as I rolled out of bed and padded into the bathroom for a quick shower. Once I was clean and dressed, I grabbed my keys and gray herringbone coat and left the house.

The drive downtown was quick, even with the early stages of morning rush hour traffic. I only lived a few miles away from the building where my office was located, one of the biggest reasons I'd chosen the house in the previously run-down neighborhood while it was affordable for me during the housing market crash a decade ago. These days, most of the houses on my street had been snapped up by young up-and-comers who brought dying houses back to life. I could have easily sold my house for half again as much as I'd paid for it even without any repairs or upgrades.

I parked in the open-air lot across the street from my building, and then stepped out to look up at the window where my office was. My plan had been to head in and check my messages for responses to some calls I'd placed late the day before, but my stomach was grumbling. For the first time in months, I felt like I was ready to return to the small café in La Villita that had long been my favorite place to enjoy breakfast.

The waitress who had served me for half a year turned out to be the lamia stealing kids from playgrounds. An unknown number of years ago, her husband's mistress had grown angry with his refusal to leave his family. In retaliation, she burned the house down with his wife and nine children inside. The kids died in the fire, but the wife survived and was reborn as a Nox, imbued by the Chaos energy left over from the formation of the universe. As part of her curse, she developed an insatiable hunger every ten years that could only be sated by devouring children. Eight girls and one boy, the same as the children she lost in that fire.

In the early stages of the case, I had latched onto a lead that all the abducted girls shared a similar uncommon blood type. Blood left behind by the lamia had later revealed that she shared that same type, something that would have been passed down to her children. It was a reminder for me that even the most mundane leads could reveal a motive behind a supernatural creature's choice of victims.

After tracking her down, she was seconds away from ripping me apart when Ollie Williams, my friend in the SAPD, arrived and shot her. She died taking so many secrets to her grave, but the girls had lived and been reunited with their families.

After all of that, I'd felt uncomfortable any time I thought about returning to the café. As if they'd know I was responsible for the death of the waitress who never returned to work. Surely some of her coworkers had thought of her as a friend. I was sure the cops had been by to question the other workers about her, while trying to figure out how she'd managed to abduct eight children from crowded playgrounds without anyone seeing her. That was something I still hadn't figured out myself.

This morning, though, I felt so good that I was more than willing to risk it. I missed my favorite breakfast of fluffy pancakes, perfectly cooked bacon, and scrambled eggs that were just on the right side of being fully cooked. For years, that calm hour most mornings had been my favorite part of the day, and I was ready to have that back.

I ducked my head and pulled my coat closer around my body as I turned and headed for the historic village close to the heart of downtown. It was too early for tourists, especially on a Wednesday morning in February. The weekend was when the crowds would descend, celebrating Valentine's Day at the many restaurants along the Riverwalk. The day that celebrated love was big business, the best day since New Year's for many of the establishments.

The bell over the door jangled as I entered the café, and I paused to enjoy the warm air that washed over me as I stood just inside. A handful of patrons were already seated, and a young man wearing a blue apron was refilling coffee cups. He looked over at me with a smile as he told me to sit anywhere I'd like.

Okay, so maybe I'd been foolish to think there could be a grudge against me. They probably didn't know I was involved in the waitress's disappearance at all. I'd made sure her body with its scaly legs and wide mouth full of sharp teeth and very long tongue was never found.

My usual table was vacant, near the window where I could look out on the cobbled pedestrian road and see a small portion of the main square. All but deserted this morning, it gave me a feeling of inner peace to soak in the sight. A minute later the waiter arrived at my table, sliding a menu in front of me. I smiled up at him and placed my regular order without even looking at it.

Learning my lesson from the waitress, I made sure to note Mark's name tag. I also took in his features, from his short, bleached hair to his tan skin that spoke of someone who enjoyed being outdoors as much as possible. If I passed him in the street, I'd assume he was one of the California transplants moving to Texas in the thousands, though most of them were relocating to Austin, an hour north on the interstate. His voice told me he was local, and probably had a close Hispanic relative who taught him Spanish growing up. The slight trace of an accent was underlying all the words.

By the time my breakfast arrived, I was famished. The salmon and asparagus I'd managed to passably put out for the date the night before had long ago been burned off. I'd only eaten small bites of it, so nervous about having Karen in my home. I scarfed down the pancakes, eggs, and bacon in half the time I usually lingered over them. When my plate was clean, I sat back, feeling full and happy as I looked out over the increasing pedestrian traffic. In that moment, everything was right in the world and I felt like nothing could ruin my day.

As happens so often, I was rudely reminded that tempting fate was a fool's game. My phone was sitting on the edge of the table, where I could see the screen as I read a book about the history of Shackleton's South Pole voyages. The screen flashed, a blue border appearing as a message popped up on top for a few seconds. Long enough for me to see it was from Ollie. I switched over to my text messages to read it, thinking he might be asking me about my date with Karen the night before.

Body in Stone Oak. You need to see this. Pretty sure it's one of yours.

I read the message several times. Ollie was one of the few humans in San Antonio who knew about the supernatural Nox who shared our world. He knew exactly what kind of things I dealt with as one of the Nine, and always let me know if he came across something that could be related during his job. I trusted his instincts after working together so long.

I dropped some cash on the table to cover my meal and a decent tip, and then waved to Mark the waiter as I left the café. At least now I didn't have to feel shy about going back most mornings. I could get back into my normal routine again. When you dealt with some of the freaky things I saw on my job, you'd be craving at least one normal hour of the day, too.

I debated running up to my office to check my laptop for messages on the other small cases I was working, but as I was approaching the parking lot my phone buzzed in my hand. I looked at the screen to see another message from Ollie, this time giving me an address of the crime scene. I copied it into my map program, checking to see how long it would take to get there. With rush hour, I was looking at a thirty-minute drive.

Deciding the laptop messages could wait, I hopped back into my trusty Honda and started it up. It wasn't as cold as the forecast had called for, but it was still chilly enough that I was happy to click the button that turned on my seat warmer. By the time I was pulling onto 281, my butt was starting to feel nice and toasty.

There was an accident near the exit to get onto Loop 1604, slowing me down and adding ten minutes to my trip. I could only curse the rubberneckers who made the delay even longer, the people who couldn't help but drive slower and watch any amount of carnage with fascinated faces. Fortunately, this time it was nothing more than a fender bender with the drivers standing outside their cars talking to the cop who had arrived to take the report.

Once I arrived in the Stone Oak neighborhood, I had to navigate a maze of streets and subdivisions to find the crime scene. As soon as I turned onto the correct street, I could see the police cars and yellow tape ahead of me. A news van was parked nearby, as well, but it wasn't Karen's station. Knowing how she kept her junior reporters on their toes, one of them had already been and gone with the scoop on the story.

I saw a familiar figure standing just in front of the yellow tape, leaning against one of the patrol cars. The young woman was a foot shorter than my own six feet, best described as petite as long as you weren't saying it to her face. Her dark brown, almost black, hair was tucked neatly under her SAPD ball cap with only a few loose strands blowing in the breeze. When I parked my car nearby, she turned honey brown eyes in my direction.

"Hey, Annie," I called as I stepped out of my warm car. I smiled brightly and waved at her, getting only a glare in return. She was a rookie, only three months into the job. Her first training officer had been forced into long-term disability a month into her training, and Ollie was the only senior officer qualified to take over. I'd met her half a dozen times since, but she had never yet warmed up to me. Ollie kept telling me the mere fact that she noticed me at all meant she liked me.

"What do you want, Dahlish? This is a crime scene."

"Yeah, Ollie wanted me to come out and take a look."

Anne Bishop snorted, turning away with a frown. The only time I hadn't seen a frown on her face was the night that Ollie and I had pulled the eight little girls from the lamia's home. She'd actually had a neutral expression that time, a contemplative look as she appraised me.

"Jack!" I turned in the direction of the voice and saw an African American man in his mid-fifties waving from the door of the house. His hair and mustache were mostly gray, his face covered in fine wrinkles and laugh lines. Ollie was one of the best people I'd ever known, and even after a decade I'd never seen him angry with anyone.

I left Annie behind, ducking under the caution tape and walking up the concrete driveway to where a short path led to a solid wooden door. While I slipped little plastic covers over my shoes and put on latex gloves, Ollie told me about what was waiting inside.

"This is a weird one, Jack. We got an anonymous call around two in the morning, someone saying we should perform a welfare check on the occupant of this address. A pair of uniforms drove by ten minutes later and rang the doorbell, but the house was dark, and no one answered. After shift change, another car stopped in. The early morning sun provided enough illumination to let them see through the windows, though, and once they saw the body they forced entry." He pointed to the narrow window beside the door, with only a gauzy curtain covering it inside the house. Thanks to the low sun shining directly through a window at the back of the house, I could see movement behind it even standing several feet away.

Ollie waved for me to follow, leading the way into the house. I nodded at the uniformed officer standing just inside as we passed. I got a scowl in return, which was depressingly common. Most of the police force hated private investigators and saw us as only a small step above ambulance chasing lawyers.

Past the foyer, we entered a short hallway which quickly opened up into a large living room and kitchen. An island separated the two spaces, creating a dividing line between the granite countertops and gleaming stainless appliances of the kitchen and the dark leather furniture and wood floors in the living room. The corpse was lying on a couch, a desiccated husk that I would have expected to find after opening a three-thousand-year-old sarcophagus buried deep under the Egyptian desert. The flesh looked more leathery than the furniture, shrunken and shiny smooth over the skull and bones. The body was wearing a t-shirt and gym shorts but looked swamped in them with its shrunken state.

"How long has this guy been dead?" I asked, releasing the pinch on my nostrils when I realized there would be no decomposition stench at this scene.

"That's the reason I wanted you here," Ollie said, leaning in to whisper the words so the crime scene people working around the body wouldn't hear. "Neighbors on the street say they just saw the guy working in his lawn two nights ago. Pulling weeds and such. One couple passed him pushing their toddler in a stroller, and he waved and spoke to them. He was wearing the same clothing."

I stared at the modern-day mummy in confusion. There was no way someone could turn into that after less than two days. No natural way, that is. This had to be the product of a Nox attack, but there was only one way to be sure.

"Any way we can clear the house for a few minutes? Let me do my thing?"

Ollie grunted. He knew the basics of how I worked, even if he wouldn't let me explain it to him in detail. At the same time, I knew I was asking a lot from him. He was a sergeant with the SAPD, and the uniformed officers would listen to him. The crime scene techs and the detective watching from the dining room table he was sitting at while making notes would not.

"Hey, I had to ask," I told him with a wan smile. This was not going to be fun with so many people around. I walked over to lean against a solid wall, just to make sure I didn't sway around when the effects hit me. The last thing I needed was the cops around us thinking I'd come to the scene hammered.

Taking a deep breath and closing my eyes, I reached up and rubbed my fingers over the talisman under my shirt. Then I opened my senses to the powers it granted. Immediately, I felt a wave of nausea and dizziness overwhelm me. It was the kind of thing you feel after eating way too many sweets, when your body is protesting while you beg every power in the universe to keep you from throwing up. Not pleasant, and I felt it every time I used the talisman.

When I opened my eyes, the rooms were filled with a swirl of colors. One of them was an inky black trail that had been made stronger by frequent passage. My nose was assaulted with the earthy smell of wet dirt, and a hint of the rotting flesh I'd been expecting earlier. For a moment, I was certain I'd found the type of Nox responsible for this death. Until I traced it back to one of the crime scene techs, a woman who was looking back at me with squinted eyes. Where I'd seen her as a healthy woman with rich dark skin earlier, I now saw sickly pale flesh around the mask that covered her nose and mouth. Her eyes were reddish brown, and her sparse black hair was stringy.

I was seeing her real form, the one hidden under the human mask Nox could adopt. She was a vampire.

She also shook her head once, slowly, before turning back to continue looking for anything that could help track the killer. It was her way of letting me know she wasn't responsible, and probably that it wasn't any of her kind. I was inclined to agree, having seen the gruesome results of vampire kills before, but it was still something I'd have to investigate.

Underneath the black trails and earthy smell was something else. Something more subtle. It was a sweet smell that made me think of peach blossoms even though it had been years since my last trip past a peach farm in the hill country.

The smell was enticing.

Intriguing.

Calming.

Even as I was trying to make out where that trail went, I could feel my mind clouding. I detected a faint pink streak in the air, buried under the black, and tried to force myself to focus on it as my eyes refused to cooperate.

A hand shoved my shoulder, and I snapped my head up to look at Ollie. He was standing in front of me with a concerned expression. "Jack. You okay? It looked like you were falling asleep."

I blinked a few times, looking around the room no longer filled with essence trails. No one was paying attention to me, thankfully. Rubbing a hand over my face, I tried to force my brain back into gear. I felt groggy and slow, the same way I did the rare times I fell asleep for ten or twenty minutes on the couch in the middle of the day. Not the way you want to feel while doing your job.

Ollie led me outside, and the cold air helped to bring me back to wakefulness. "What the hell just happened?" he asked, leaning in.

"I don't know. I picked up on something. It was very faint and subtle. The next thing I know I felt like I was falling asleep and I couldn't keep my attention focused on anything."

"Has that ever happened before?"

"Not to me." I shook my head one more time, clearing the last of the cobwebs. "Whatever creature was here, they might just have some kind of self-defense mechanism against the Nine." And that was a scary thought.

3

I left the crime scene a few minutes later, driving slowly as I left Stone Oak and headed back downtown. I kept copies of a lot of the books I used in my research on the Nox in my office, and I wanted to peruse a few of them. I'd never heard of anything with the ability to deflect the attention of a talisman bearer trying to detect them.

It was times like these when I regretted not being in contact with the other members of the Nine. All of them had been wearing the coins longer than I had, though I didn't know specifics. I'd asked Richard once, a friend who owned a bar that catered to Nox and knew more of the supernatural world than I did, but he'd been cagey and refused to give specific answers. He did tell me that the guy who wore my talisman before me held it for more than thirty years. That was a lot of experience I would love to be able to draw upon in situations like this.

Traffic was lighter on my return trip with rush hour having ended while I was in the house looking at the desiccated corpse and being lulled into a half sleep. It was midmorning when I parked in the lot again and crossed the street to enter my building. The 1920's construction and accents in the lobby were part of the reason I had been so excited to get even a small space in the building. The proximity to the Riverwalk and interstates was a bonus.

My small office suite was halfway up the building. The elevator opened onto a long hallway, with half a dozen doors on either side. This floor was divided up into mini suites for small businesses and individual operators like me. I only knew a few of my neighbors; one woman was a fashion designer who used the small suite to test out ideas in private, and a man at the end of the hall was a shyster lawyer who seemed to only get one client a week. It was perfect for me, since no one ever asked me questions about the people who visited my office.

Opening the door from the hallway brought me into my small reception room. I had half a dozen chairs, a couple of end tables, and a scattering of old magazines. The newest was a *Conde Nast* that I'd spitefully stolen from a law office higher in the building a month earlier during a case. The room was covered in a light film of dust, evidence of how rarely it was used.

The door at the opposite end of the reception area opened onto my larger but still cramped office. I had a cheap but presentable wooden desk, with two thinly padded chairs on the near side for clients and a comfortable but stunningly expensive swivel chair on the other for myself. Several secure file cabinets were against one wall, opposite a heavy steel door that protected a small closet where I stored dangerous or sensitive items recovered during my various cases. That room was more secure than most bank vaults.

As I settled into my comfortable chair, my eyes happened to land on a string of six childish drawings hanging on the wall beside the entry. Penny Castillo, the little girl I'd been hired to find a few months earlier, had become a fixture in my life. Unlike most clients, who I almost never saw again once I finished a job, Penny and her family had made an effort to show their appreciation for what I'd done. I'd become attached to the little

20

girl, and often babysat so her parents could get time alone. Whenever she visited my office, she insisted on drawing me a new picture to hang on the wall.

When my eyes moved past the drawings that always made me smile, I jumped in shock. There was a man leaning against the wall with arms crossed over his chest, occupying the corner of the office that couldn't be seen by anyone entering. He was tall, close to my six feet, with a thin frame. He was wearing blue jeans, with a white button-up shirt tucked tightly into them. A dark gray waistcoat completed the ensemble. His sleeves were rolled up to his elbows, exposing arms that were covered in intricate tattoos. He had vivid red hair, cut short and pushed up at the front over his clean-shaven face.

"It's about time you got to work," he said with a slight Irish brogue and a playful grin.

"I've been working for a couple of hours," I said defensively, trying to figure out who this guy could be. "What are you doing in my office? Who are you?"

He reached up to tap his chest, and at the same moment I felt a pulse of heat from the coin laying against mine. "You really should learn how to use that properly," he said as he walked over to plop down in one of my client chairs. "And the whole private investigator thing? Isn't that a bit of a cliché, fella?"

"It pays the bills," I said slowly, still amazed at what had just happened. "You're one of the Nine?"

"Aye, and you should have felt me before you even entered the building. I sensed you coming for a good five minutes before you walked through the door."

I reached up to touch my coin, still feeling the warmth that had radiated from it. The only other time I'd felt such a thing was when I was in mortal danger and the talisman acted to protect me. "How did you do that?"

He shook his head in bemusement. "I know the others don't like how you came by the coin, but they really should have reached out to give you some training." He leaned forward, holding out his fist. "I'm Padraig Reilly. If you ever call me Paddy, I'll kill ya."

I bumped his knuckles with my own. "Jack Dahlish."

"Aye, I know all about you, Jack. You come up often at our meetings over the last ten years."

"Meetings? What meetings?"

He had the grace to look a little embarrassed. "The Nine hold meetings every few years. Share knowledge, tell old war stories, that kind of thing."

I was dumbfounded. "No one ever told me any of this. I've never even spoken to any of you except one time when Angel passed through town. He said maybe five sentences the entire time."

Padraig laughed and nodded. "Angel is a man of few words at the best of times. Get a little vodka in him, though, and the man opens up like a flower." He reached up to rub the back of his head. "Look, I'd love to sit here and chat with you all day, but I'm in a bit of a pickle and I need some help."

It was hard for me to hold back the flood of questions I had. All these years wearing the talisman, and never a chance to speak with another member of the Nine. I'd always assumed that was just the way they worked, and now I'd learned I was being left out on purpose. Finally, I decided that my best bet to get answers was to help him with whatever he needed and earn them. "What kind of help?"

"I've been on the trail of a particularly dangerous Nox for several months now. I've tracked it through Europe, into Asia, across the Pacific, and now all the way to your fair city. I have a good idea of where the creature is holed up, but I'm not familiar enough with the area to go in searching for it alone."

"What are we talking about here? Pretty rare for Nox to travel that far, isn't it?"

"Oh, it happens. Especially when they kill a family in Dublin, and I swear a blood oath to put them down." Padraig's face was hard, his expression one of vengeance. "Have you ever heard of the jotnar?"

I shook my head. "Doesn't even sound familiar. What are they?"

He pulled out his phone, the latest Apple model, quickly typed in a query, and then slid it across the desk to me. I saw an image of an amorphous figure above several paragraphs of text. Perusing it, I found out that jotnar was the plural form for jotunn. They were giants from Norse mythology, where several gods were said to be jotunn. Odin himself was descended from them in some forms of the myths.

"Wow," I said, passing the phone back across the desk. "That looks like an imposing creature."

"Ay, that he is. I thought I had him in Hyderabad, sprung a trap on him that would have succeeded against almost any other creature. But the jotunn shrugged it off and got away. Left behind my shattered dignity, and also put me in a hospital for quite a while before I could pick up his trail again."

I considered it for a few minutes. According to the entry I'd just read, accounts varied on what exactly the jotunn were. Some myths called them giants, while others described them as similar to trolls. I'd been up against trolls a few times in my career, and narrowly escaped each fight. But there was one person I knew would be able to help me out as I tried to assist Padraig. I pulled out a notepad from my desk drawer, writing down directions.

"Meet me here at five o'clock. It's a place called Lyon's Den, but there aren't any signs. If you have trouble finding it, call me and I'll meet you at one of the tourist spots to guide you in."

"Nox hangout, is it? Those places are always a pain to find. I hope they have good beer. It's been ages since I've had anything but Guinness. Bartenders hear the accent and think it's a taste of home or some shite."

We bumped fists again before he sauntered out of my office, and I watched him leave with trepidation. I was hoping he showed up at the Den that evening, and I didn't miss my chance to finally get more answers about the talisman around my neck. I found my hand wrapped around it when I shook myself from my thoughts.

"Enough daydreaming, Dahlish. Get to work."

The first thing I did was pick up my phone and scroll through the Contacts list. I found the number I was searching for, pressed the button to dial it, and then waited until I got voice mail. I left a quick message, asking my friend to meet me at the Den later that afternoon, mentioning there was work involved.

That done, I opened my laptop lid to check the few messages that came in overnight and begin my searches for what kind of creature could drain a body and leave behind a desiccated husk in less than thirty-six hours. There were a lot of possibilities to wade through.

4

A few hours into my research, a chime from my phone pulled my nose out of a book on Japanese myths. Because there was no repository of information from previous wearers of the talisman, I had to look at the only other source I knew of – old mythology. A surprisingly large number of myths and fairy tales were based on real encounters with Nox in the distant past. Usually in the days before they started to hide themselves behind masks to keep the growing human population from hunting them to extinction.

I picked up my phone and found a message from Karen. Just seeing her name on the screen made me feel like a giddy teenager. I'd thought for sure that feeling would begin to fade, but two months after meeting her I still felt it as strongly as ever. Stronger than I'd ever felt it for any other girlfriend.

I know you're working through lunch. Eat!

My stomach rumbled at that moment, reminding me that it had been a long time since breakfast. I chuckled, loving how well she knew me and could guess at what I was doing. I tapped on the keypad, sending off a reply.

Guilty. Want to grab something with me?

The truth was that I knew her just as well these days. Karen would spend her mornings in bed after working late the night before, unless some juicy story gave her a reason to be up early. Around noon, she would wake up and immediately check with the station for the latest updates on what had happened during the night and morning. Despite anchoring the five and ten o'clock news almost every night, Karen still insisted on working as a roving reporter for the big stories.

The place with the eggrolls. Give me thirty to put my face on.

Bounding out of my chair, I grabbed the gray herringbone and swung it around to push my arms into the sleeves. Two minutes later, I was walking out of the building and looking both ways before jogging across the street to the parking lot. I knew exactly which place she was talking about, an Asian restaurant that we had passed on our second date and both professed to love. They made some of the best eggrolls in town, and the rest of the menu was fantastic, as well.

I made it across town in fifteen minutes, parking in the shady lot of the compact shopping center where the restaurant was located earlier than expected. Leaning my head back, I ran through my list of possible creatures for the killing.

First were the vampires. I'd detected a new family of them during a case two months earlier and hadn't taken time to follow up on that and check in with them. Unlike most other Nox, vampires tended to be very territorial. Most cities couldn't handle more than one or two families without some kind of fight breaking out between them, and this was now the third group in San Antonio. They had taken over a vacant area, coincidentally that which had previously been occupied by the clutch that went wild with bloodlust and managed to kill the last man to wear my talisman.

However, vampires rarely drained a victim of all their blood. When they did, what was left behind was a pale corpse, not a desiccated husk. For the most part, vampires used their seductive powers and immense wealth to build a stable of willing donors to feed from whenever the cravings became too strong. Most of them could go a week or more between feedings and were satisfied with no more than half a liter. The same amount you would lose during a donation at the Blood Mobile. That, and the presence of a vampire as part of the crime scene group, made me think of them as an option of last resort.

The second possibility was a wraith. They were rare creatures, solitary hunters that had never chosen to adapt human disguises. Instead, they roamed the world as insubstantial wisps and were often mistaken for ghosts when witnessed by the unlucky few. Most who saw them did not survive to tell the tale, dying horribly as their life force and soul were drained from their body over long, agonizing minutes. As far as I knew, I'd never come across a wraith's trail and there were none in San Antonio. With a creature that can hide in the slightest shadow, though, you never knew where one could be.

A third option was Lamashtu, a demoness from Mesopotamian mythology. Much like Lamia from the Greek myths, it was possible that Lamashtu was representative of a type of Nox rather than a single person. She was said to have abducted and drained pregnant women and breastfeeding children. So probably not involved in this case of a dead man, unless the myths were way off on the types of victim. Nonetheless, her chosen method of draining the bodies of blood put her on my list.

Last, and least feasible, was the chupacabra. Laugh all you want, but one of the creatures went feral several years ago and sightings of it popped up all over the place a few hours southeast of town. Animalistic Nox, the chupacabras appeared as normal dogs most of the time. Angry dogs, the kind that would snarl at any humans walking by. They were usually adopted as pets by Nox families, who treated them more like an honored guest. Comfortable beds, the choicest cuts of meat, and all the pampering any dog owner would wish they could provide. In return, the chupacabra would protect the family from any threats.

Chupacabra were pack hunters from the old days before Spanish conquistadors arrived in the New World to begin forcing their religion and diseases down native throats. These days, they tended to attack and drink the blood of livestock. Usually goats, for some reason I could never find an explanation of. That only happened if the chupacabra was left alone and uncared for, however. Given the desirability of them among the Nox families of South Texas and Mexico, I thought it would be pretty rare to find another one abandoned so soon after the last.

There were other options, especially a few from Japanese and Chinese myths that were basically vampires with different origins, but I put them down as possibilities that could be checked out if my first options failed to provide a lead.

A knock on the window startled me, and I opened my eyes to look over at a smiling face. Karen shook her head as she crooked her finger at me. I slid out of the dwindling warmth of my car, wrapping my arms around her in a hug as our lips met.

"What were you thinking about so deeply?" she asked after the kiss, as we walked toward the restaurant with our hands linked together.

"Ollie called me in on something this morning, and I'm trying to come up with possible suspects for it."

Karen pursed her lips, tapping a slim finger against them. "Let me guess. The mummified body out in Stone Oak?"

I laughed, chiding myself for not expecting her to already know all about it. "That's the one. I was pretty sure there was already a Nox involved from the state of the body, but the essence trail confirmed it."

The moment we stepped into the restaurant, the man behind the host/hostess stand fell all over himself to make sure Karen was taken care of. It was something I'd come to expect when I was out in public with the beautiful redheaded reporter. Few men seemed able to resist her charms, and even quite a few women were entranced from the moment they saw her.

We got a great table near a bay window, looking out onto a small but peaceful Zen garden. I wondered how often it was tended, and by whom. The gurgle of the water from a fountain was audible through the glass, and it was definitely creating a feeling of serenity within me.

The waitress was at our table quickly, taking drink orders and hovering over Karen as she talked about the dishes she'd recommend. I could only smile and shake my head as I sat ignored until I hastily added in my own order as the waitress started to walk away. When you dated someone from television, you got used to being almost irrelevant.

While we waited, Karen thanked me for the fabulous date the night before. She was being kind when she told me I'd cooked one of the best meals she'd ever eaten, especially since the asparagus came out of a bag.

"I still can't believe you've never seen the old Frankenstein and Dracula movies before."

"It wasn't something we did when I was growing up," she said with a smile.

Leaning forward in interest, I sensed that it might be a good time to ask about her childhood. In all the times we'd been together, she rarely talked about anything from the days before she came to San Antonio twelve years earlier to begin her reporting career. "What did you do as a kid, if you didn't get to watch scary old movies?"

"My sister and I spent a lot of time reading or playing board games. We moved around a lot, so we never really got to have close friends outside of the family."

"Sister? Tell me about her. Younger or older?"

Karen paused, biting her lip as she looked into my eyes. "Younger, by three years. I haven't seen her since I went out on my own. It's funny, I don't usually even talk about her. But she called me a couple of nights ago, saying she'll be passing through town and wanted to spend a few nights on my couch."

"That's awesome," I said, reaching out to take her hand. "I bet you'll love getting to see her again."

"Maybe," she said hesitantly. The food arrived at that moment, and as soon as the server walked away, she changed the subject before I could follow up with more questions. "So, what kind of Nox do you think could be responsible for your mummy?"

I told her about the things I'd found during my research, and about the vampire working as a crime scene tech. She laughed when I told her about the chupacabra, convinced I was making that up until I assured her I was serious. "Trust me, I spent two weeks camping in dusty fields tracking that thing down before it could move from killing livestock to killing people. I had to go in and get a rabies shot after I was done, because the damn thing got its teeth into my arm."

"You said there are three vampire families," she said between bites of orange chicken. "Maybe that crime scene person was just telling you it wasn't her family."

"Yeah, I've thought about that. I don't even know which clutch she belongs to. Keeping track of vampires is not something I look forward to, especially after they killed my predecessor. I guess this gives me the excuse I need to go meet the newcomers, though."

We spent the next fifteen minutes talking about vampires, with Karen asking me how the real ones compared to those in books like *Twilight* and *Interview With A Vampire*. Short version – no sparkles, they're not all drop dead gorgeous, and they can go out in daylight just fine. The last one was the biggest disappointment for her. It was one of the oldest traits attributed to the creatures, which Karen thought made it the safest thing to believe.

"And there was an essence beneath the vampire trail? What was that one like?"

I chewed a piece of shrimp thoughtfully, trying to find the best way to put it into words. "It was sweet, both in smell and taste. Soothing, almost, since it put me into a trance just from being near it. Pink shades mixed with a deeper red as it got closer to the body."

Karen's face had gone even more pale than usual as I talked, and she coughed as she choked on her bite of chicken. She washed it down with a big sip of iced tea, and then patted her napkin over her mouth.

"You okay?" I asked.

"Fine. Just went down wrong," she replied with a strange smile. For a moment, I worried that maybe I'd said something wrong. But she put her hand on top of mine, and her cool touch reassured me that everything was alright.

Karen told me about the story she was working on for the night's broadcasts. It was a happy story, about a couple of young kids in elementary school who had won a nationwide contest. Their prizes were free trips to Washington D.C. to meet with a couple of senators and get a tour of the White House.

After we paid the bill, I walked Karen back to her car. Her smile was still a bit strange, but I put it down to talking about a murder victim over lunch. Even the most hardened of people could be uncomfortable when something like that came up. Especially when you couldn't help thinking of dried figs every time you thought about the body you'd seen only that morning. I didn't know if I'd ever eat another fig again.

I got a brief kiss before she ducked into her little red sportscar, waving as she drove away. Walking over to my Honda, I felt lighter and more relaxed than I had before lunch. I might not have any hard suspects to go after, but I could start with the vampire families and see where that led me.

5

I decided to begin with the woman from the crime scene. She would most likely still be at work, which made her easy to track down. I had very little experience with the vampire families in town, aside from knowing who the heads of the families were and seeing a few members at Lyon's Den every rare now and then.

It was a short drive over to the Medical Center, where the nondescript brick building that housed the forensics group was nestled amid hospitals, clinics, and nursing schools. There was little signage telling people what the building was for, and I always wondered how many of the people who worked nearby even realized crime-solving efforts were underway inside.

On the drive, I called Ollie and managed to get him on the phone. He was sitting in the patrol car, soaking in warmth while his rookie directed traffic around an accident scene. He gave me the name of the woman I'd seen earlier that morning, Mariah Mathis. He was familiar with her from other crime scenes, and said he'd reach out to see if she could spare me a few minutes. Thankfully, he didn't ask why I wanted to see her. I didn't want to have to explain to Ollie how one of the people he worked with was a vampire. That would just make it awkward for him in the future. I liked to respect the privacy of the Nox whenever I could, especially those who were holding to the Covenants and not causing any trouble.

I parked outside the building, having to painfully navigate my car into a parallel parking space since the other visitor spots were already full. I detested parallel parking more than almost anything else in the world, and I would drive around a block ten times to avoid it if I could. I considered doing that here, but when I looked toward the building, I saw Mariah through the glass. She was staring out at the parking lot, an anxious expression on her face. I felt sure that she was wondering why I would have asked to speak with her directly.

As soon as I climbed out of my Honda, I felt her eyes snap over to me. I looked up and our eyes met. Giving her a small nod to try and convey peaceful intentions, I walked up the steps and pulled open the glass door.

The lobby was deserted aside from the two of us. I looked around, though, and saw several small cameras covering every inch of the space. I couldn't take the chance of some bored security guard happening to eavesdrop on our conversation at the wrong time. I greeted Mariah with a smile. "Thanks for meeting with me, Ms. Mathis. I just have some questions about the crime scene this morning. Would you like to walk down the street and get a coffee with me?"

There was a local coffee shop not far down the road. It would give us a long walk, time to talk in the open without eavesdroppers. Mariah agreed, glancing around the lobby for a few seconds before walking out of the building with me.

"I promise I have no intention of screwing things up for you," I said as soon as we were in the open air. "I really do just need more information about that corpse."

She visibly relaxed. Asking her to talk outside of the building helped, since it showed I didn't want any of her co-workers to hear what we said. It let her know I wasn't going to expose her secret, not that doing so would be any better for me than it would be for her. "Thank you, Mr. Dahlish. I've been worrying since I felt your attention on me this morning."

"Call me Jack, please. You could feel it when I had my senses open?" That was a surprise to me. I knew that some Nox seemed able to perceive when I could see their true appearance, but I'd only encountered that during fights or while confronting dangerous people. I'd put it down to their hyper vigilance or paranoia in the moment.

"It felt like someone walking over my grave," she said, with a small smile. "It's not a strong feeling, but kind of like a cool breeze that didn't stop blowing until you looked away."

That was information I wish I'd known during the last ten years. How many Nox had eluded me longer than they might have because I was opening myself to the talisman's powers when I shouldn't have? Was there a way to refine that, and make it impossible for them to realize what I was doing? Two more questions added to the inexhaustible list I was building for Padraig.

"Which clutch do you belong to, Mariah? Ollie said you've been working here for a few years, so you can't be with the new family."

She grimaced at the mention of the latest arrivals. "I belong to the Harrison family," she said proudly. That was a name I knew. The Harrison clutch, under patriarch Uriah Harrison, controlled the southeastern part of the city. As far as I knew, they were the most powerful vampire family in San Antonio.

"I met Uriah once. Seemed like a decent guy, but he has to be in his eighties by now, right?"

She laughed, a rich sound that rolled out smoothly. "He's almost a hundred and fifty, Jack. Our lifespans are twice what a human can expect. With luck, he'll be around for another twenty or thirty years."

Okay, so I didn't know as much about vampires as I should have. At least I had known they weren't the immortals always portrayed in films. Nothing lives forever in this world, not even the gods. "What's your opinion about our dead guy this morning? Could a vampire have done something like that?"

"Never," Mariah said adamantly. "Even if we give in to the bloodlust and drain a person dry, the body would never be left in such a withered condition."

"Even the other families? I know each clutch of vampires has slightly different traits. Maybe the newbies leave their victims in such a state."

She shook her head, sending her loose hair flying. "They wouldn't dare to hunt in Stone Oak. That area belongs to the Van Owen family. They have everything east of I-10 to I-35, all the way up to State Highway 46."

"Okay, but the Van Owen family are pretty reclusive. Maybe the new clutch thinks that makes them weak and ripe for expansion."

Mariah grunted, but thought about it for a while before answering. "Have you met the new group yet, Jack?"

"No. I found out about them a couple of months ago, but I've been too busy with work to track them down to do a meet and greet."

"They're... strange. Especially for vampires. We have no idea where they came from before they arrived in San Antonio, for one thing. Uriah has reached out to his contacts all over North America, and he can't find anyone with knowledge of them."

That was definitely odd. Vampires were well known to generate vast information webs. After several years of service, their most favored blood donor volunteers would be given resources to create businesses in any area the patriarch or matriarch felt there was a gap in their far-flung network. In return, that donor provided information and a small cut of their profits. It was an agreement that proved mutually beneficial, and almost always increased the power of the clutch. For them to have no knowledge of the new family was strange, indeed.

"Not only that," Mariah said quietly. "They haven't advertised for donors. As far as we can tell, they aren't getting their blood from anywhere. Even the blood clinics haven't been contacted about providing some bags."

I was getting an uneasy feeling about this new group of vampires. Tracking them down moved way up on my to-do list, especially if they could be involved in this latest killing.

We arrived at the coffee shop, and I held the door for Mariah. There were a handful of students from the nearby campus seated at tables, all of them with a laptop open in front of them as they worked on papers or research. Most had headphones over their ears, but you could never tell if they were listening to music or just wanted to prevent someone from bothering them.

Once we got our coffees, we took a table in the corner. I considered one of the small tables outside for more privacy, but my hands were already freezing from the walk. I turned the subject to safer territory. "What have you guys discovered about the body so far?"

Mariah looked at me with a raised eyebrow. "It's only been three hours since we left Stone Oak, Jack."

"I know, TV always makes it look so much easier than it really is. Have you verified it's really the guy who lived in the house, at least?" I was half hoping she'd say it wasn't, and it would turn out to be some old body that was decades dead and naturally mummified.

"Oh, it was definitely him. Our guy had a couple of really old tattoos from when he served in Vietnam. We had to stretch out the skin a bit to be sure, but markings on the body match. It'll be a few days before we get DNA confirmation."

"How about a tox report? Is that being done?"

"It's on the list, and the results should be in tomorrow or the next day. At this point, we're more concerned with figuring out what caused his body to shrivel up so much, and so quickly."

"Join the club," I said with a smile, taking a sip of my coffee. It was surprisingly good, less bitter than what I usually got at big chain locations, with an aftertaste that was pleasant on the tongue. "Anything that might help us with a timeline? Ollie said some neighbors saw him in the yard a few nights ago, but that's still a big gap to try and work with."

Mariah nodded, leaning forward. "We found a receipt in his kitchen. Food delivery from last night, and he had to sign for it. That signature matches others we found on papers in the home."

"Okay, that's something I can work with. Could you tell me where the delivery was from? Maybe I can track the driver down and ask them some questions."

"The detectives took the receipt as soon as we found it. They're already on that, and they don't like to share information with us science geeks." She grinned with the words, her white teeth bright against her dark skin. For a moment, my brain flashed back to how she'd looked under that veil, and I had to suppress a shudder.

"At least it's something to work with." I looked around the shop, trying to wipe the disturbing image from my mind before I turned back to her. "So, what makes a vam... uh, someone like you decide to pursue a career in criminology?"

She shrugged, leaning back in her chair again. Her face lost the excitement that had filled it as we talked about the case. "Uriah needed people on the inside. We have a couple of cops already, but with the rise of forensic sciences he decided it was time to get in there, as well. I've always been fascinated with physics and chemistry, so I volunteered. Better to have one of us working there than to depend on a donor."

"That actually makes sense. Do the Van Owen family have someone there, as well? Can you work with someone from a rival family?"

That made her laugh, but it was almost bitter. "They tried to get someone in, but their candidate failed the interview process. Uriah makes me work with them when they pay him enough for information."

More interesting details. I was learning more about vampires during a quick coffee run than I had in the last ten years. I needed to get out from behind my desk more often and talk with the Nox in the real world instead of burying my nose in books of tales from centuries past.

"And you're okay with that?"

"It's not the greatest situation, but I don't mind too much." Mariah leaned forward again, lowering her voice. "You're seeing us a rivals, Jack, fighting over territory. But that's not how the families operate. Once we define our areas, it's rare for a patriarch or matriarch to decide to try expanding into another family's part of town. The families are small, and we have more than enough resources in our areas to sustain us."

I had to remind myself that the resources she was talking about were humans. People with blood pumping through their veins who could be paid or seduced into becoming willing victims to feed the vampires. Many of them came out of it with more wealth and privilege than they could have expected to gain in a normal life, but some were left utterly broken by the experience. If you ever happen to visit a mental institution, pay attention to how many of the patients scream about blood suckers.

"That's good to know. I can stop expecting a vampire war to break out." I smiled to let her know I was kidding.

She made a face. "No, thank you. I've heard stories about the last one, and I don't want to be part of that." I made a mental note to ask for that story sometime.

We drained the last of our coffees and began the walk back to the crime lab building. Back in the open air, I felt comfortable wading into strange waters again. "This new clutch. Do you know where I could find them?"

Mariah sighed, shaking her head. "Not a clue. We know they're based in the Far West Side somewhere, but that's all we've been able to learn. Uriah and Emily have agreed to leave them be as long as they stick to the territory the Werner family occupied before their downfall."

The Harrison patriarch and Van Owen matriarch were obviously in contact, then. And friendly enough to make such agreements. "What, uh, territory exactly?"

Mariah smirked at me. "Shouldn't you know that already, Mr. Talisman Bearer?"

"Probably, but I'm finding my vampire knowledge to be very deficient lately."

"West of I-10 all the way down to I-35 south of downtown. Back in the eighties when the territory boundaries were last decided, it was a pretty empty area, but it's grown a lot since then."

"I know the Far West Side is a hot part of town right now, but wasn't it still pretty populated forty years ago? Sea World started a lot of expansion in that direction."

"I meant the 1880's, Jack." She was smiling effortlessly, at ease around me now that she wasn't worried that I was there trying to tie her in with the murder. "The boundaries shifted a bit when the interstates were built in the middle of the last century, but the change was surprisingly minimal."

"Ah. I guess that makes more sense. Let me guess, Uriah's father was the Harrison patriarch back then?"

"The previous patriarch wasn't a relative, actually. Our families aren't like your human kingdoms. When our leader dies, we select the next one based on ability to keep the clutch safe."

I stopped at the bottom of the stairs leading up to the building entrance, holding out my hand while Mariah looked at it and then shook it with a grin. "I'll let you know what I find out west, if you'll let me know anything new that comes up on our mummy."

"Deal," she said, pulling out her phone and getting my number. She sent a text so I'd have her number, as well, and then waved as she walked up the steps and went back to work.

Sliding into my car, I felt proud of myself for being able to befriend another Nox. Too few of them knew me as anything more than one of the Nine, and I really did need to change that.

6

I wanted to head west right then to start searching for the new vampire clutch, but it was getting close to the time I'd set to meet with Padraig. Instead, I turned my car in the direction of downtown, and drove until I got to the lot across the street from my office building. On the way, I had time to think about everything I'd learned from Mariah. She seemed honest as she talked to me, open about some things while hesitant to talk about others. I felt like I could trust her information and drop two of the vampire families down my list of possible suspects. If the newcomers were considered strange by other vampires, though, they might have moved up to the top of my list.

As I drove, I dictated notes into my phone. I wanted to get down as much of the new information as I could, until I could type it up and print it out to store in my fireproof locked cabinets. Digital notes were too exposed if someone decided to hack my systems, so I kept everything on paper in a place where I felt it was more secure.

I strolled to the Riverwalk with my mind in the clouds, trying to figure out how I'd track down the new family of vampires. One thing was sure, I would wait until the morning to begin the search. Trying to find them at night was foolish, when I couldn't be sure they wouldn't attack me on sight while they were at the height of their strength.

Once I was down the stairs and in the flow of tourists walking the path beside the water, I had to let those thoughts go and concentrate on my surroundings. I knew the way to the Den well enough now to find it with a blindfold on, but I kept my eyes open in case I saw Padraig nearby looking confused and unable to find the entrance. It was still half an hour before our meeting time, but I hoped he would show up early so I could pepper him with questions while we waited on the third member of the party to arrive.

No such luck. I walked into Lyon's Den without seeing the Irishman. The bar was half full already, a large crowd for the middle of the week. My normal stool was vacant, and as I settled onto it the people sitting nearby got up and moved farther down the bar. It was something I was accustomed to.

I nodded at Terrance, sitting seven stools away as usual. The half-goblin Nox was a petty conman, performing small-time grifts on tourists most days. I'd been standoffish with him for years, until he did me a favor during a case a few months back and earned my trust. He actually smiled as he nodded at me this time.

The bartender sauntered over, stopping to fill a few glasses along the way. Richard Lyon was a thin man, a few inches over my six feet, with long reddish-brown hair swept back from his forehead. In the ten years that I'd known him, his look hadn't changed once. He was human, but his bar had been a Nox haven for so long that they were comfortable dropping their disguises around him the couple of nights each month that he allowed it.

"Jack, it's been a few days. How are things going?"

"Busy, Richard. Always busy. What's on tap tonight?" He always had a few kegs from a random local microbrewery available until they were empty, never repeating the same thing twice. It had been years since I drank anything else.

"A special batch in honor of Valentine's Day." He walked over to fill a tall glass to the brim, sliding it across to me.

I took a sip of the new ale, swirling it around in my mouth before swallowing. It was almost sweet, with a hint of flavor that was familiar. "Is that strawberry?"

"Bingo," he said with a smile. "Chocolate and strawberries, the perfect pairing for a day built around love."

I took another sip. It wasn't bad, and it tasted better the more I drank it. Definitely not one of my favorites, but not at the bottom of the ranks, either. "I'm going to have a couple of guests tonight, Richard. Should be here soon."

"Do you need a table?" he asked, waving at the row of them against the wall opposite the bar. Few of them were occupied, with most patrons choosing to sit at the bar.

"We'll be fine here," I said, looking at the buffer zone of empty stools that always surrounded me when I was in the bar. He nodded and walked away to help another customer, while I looked around and waited.

Ten years earlier, when I'd come into possession of the talisman around my neck, there had been a slip of paper inside that led me to the bar. Richard Lyon was the man who told me what the coin was, and who the Nine were. He explained the Filii Nox to me and told me about the powerful Relics that were created from the same Chaos energy that had formed the universe. He had one of them himself, though I'd never seen it. Few people who held Relics talked about them, or let others see them.

It was five o'clock on the dot when a large hand dropped onto my shoulder. The man who settled on a stool nearby was wide enough to fill three spots on his own. His body was pure muscle, the kind of strength that came from having a great-grandfather who had been an ogre. The height and strength of that Nox relative had skipped a few generations, and then made up for it in spades with Nyk. He worked as a bounty hunter, taking jobs for humans and Nox alike. One of the best, I often called on him when I needed help tracking someone down.

"Where's your friend?" he asked, as he waved at Richard and held up two fingers.

"Late," I said, checking my phone to be sure Padraig hadn't called for help finding the bar. The only notification was a reminder about another case I'd been working on. "Thanks for coming."

"You called at a good time. I just got back from a week in the Mexican desert tracking down a naga. Damn thing was taking money to fill wells with water, and then disappearing without doing the work."

"At least you got some warm weather for a while."

"You ever been camping in the desert on a winter night, Jack? Let me tell you, it was not the most pleasant of trips."

I thought about that, remembering that deserts can be just as cold at night as they are hot in the day. Not to mention all the creepy crawlies that you'd often find sharing your tent when you woke. Maybe Nyk was right. I was thankful he hadn't asked me to tag along on that job. At the same time, I was glad to have someone like him in my town, handling the jobs that no one would come to me with.

The bar went totally silent as the door opened. A shaft of fading sunlight filled the room for half a minute, until the new-comer stepped inside and let it slam closed behind him. I turned to see Padraig standing there, smirking around at the Nox that filled the room. He winked at them, and then sauntered over to sit on the stool on my other side.

"Nice place you have here, Dahlish. Cozy."

Richard was staring at the Irishman, almost glaring as he walked over. He gave me a reproachful look before speaking. "This bar is a safe place, sanctioned under the Covenants. You're welcome here as long as you respect the rights of my patrons."

Padraig chuckled, but nodded. "I'll be a wee good boy, bar-keep."

Richard looked him over, then nodded and turned away to fill a glass. As if they'd been waiting on his approval, the Nox around us began their conversations again. More than a few glances flickered in our direction, however.

"Padraig, this is my friend Nyk Walsh. He's a bounty hunter, and one of the best trackers in the States. I thought he could help with your problem."

The Irishman leaned forward to look around me. "How are you, big fella?"

"Curious," Nyk rumbled. "Jack said you've been after some-one for a while, through Europe and Asia, but he didn't say much else."

"Aye, I imagine he wanted to hear me tell it." Padraig winked at me as Richard set his beer down. He lifted it, holding

48

it in our direction. "Slainte." He took a deep drink, grunted, and then grinned before taking another. "That's not half bad. I'll have another one, barkeep!"

"Give us the story," I said, once he'd drained the first glass of ale and started on the second. "You didn't really tell me very much in my office this morning."

"True, I have a habit of keeping things close to me vest. Nyk, have you ever heard of the jotnar or encountered one before?"

Nyk surprised me by nodding. "Giants, according to legend, though the two I've known were smaller than me."

"I imagine most people are smaller than you," Padraig said. "But you have it right. The myths made them giants more to explain their power than because of their stature. They are closer to gods than most Nox you'll come across. Luckily, there are few of them left.

"Seven months ago, I found out one of them was living in Dublin. That's my city, and I'm responsible for keeping it safe. I went to see this fella, make sure he knew to stick to the rules. But he had a grudge from the moment we met, and not two days later a family on his street were torn to pieces." Padraig paused to take a drink.

"Mum, dad, and four wee ones. All of them ripped apart, with limbs laying all over the place. I knew right away who was responsible. He calls himself Surtr, forty-eighth of that name. I swore a blood oath then and there to see justice for that family, and there is nothing that will stop me.

"I tracked him across the sea to Wales, through England to Dover, and then across the Channel into Brussels. In a dozen cities, I found more families torn apart. Only a day or two before I arrived. More victims left behind by the jotunn as he ran from me like a coward.

"By the time I followed Surtr to India, the list of the dead was in the hundreds. In Hyderabad, I managed to coordinate with another one of the Nine, Gitna Sridhar. She and I managed to set a trap for the jotunn that should have stopped him once and for all.

"By that time, I'd found many of his previous hiding places and seen the pattern. It was always in cave systems, or houses above them where he could burrow down. So we found the largest caves near Hyderabad and hired mercenaries. There were ten of us waiting for him, carrying .50 caliber rifles that could take down a bloody elephant."

Padraig grimaced as he finished the second beer, waving for Richard to bring another. I was amazed that he showed no signs of feeling the alcohol yet.

"Surtr sprung the trap alright, but he proved to be more powerful than I'd expected. His skin was tough, like old leather. The bullets pierced it, but not very deeply. He took at least seven shots, and still barreled through us. Five of the mercenaries died. I ended up in hospital for more than a week with broken bones and head injuries. Gitna... she was still in a coma when I left."

"Your talismans didn't protect you?" I asked, thinking about the time a couple of tengu jumped me in an alley. My coin had grown blisteringly hot, shooting out a beam of light that scared them away.

"Aye, we'd both have been pulp if not for the strength from the talismans." He reached up to stroke his coin, as I often found myself doing when I thought about it. "I'd still be in hospital if not for its regenerative powers, too. I can only hope Gitna's talisman will restore her, though she hasn't responded to any of my messages."

"Whoa. Regenerative powers?" I touched my talisman, wondering if it had healed me in the past and turned significant injuries into minor nuisances.

Padraig looked at me with a bemused smile. "Just a babe in the woods, you are. Anyway, after I left hospital in India, I managed to track Surtr through southern Asia. He was killing more frequently now. Once, I found an entire village destroyed by his wrath. Thirty-four people disappeared in the night, not a trace of their bodies ever found.

"Through Singapore, Indonesia, into Australia. He kept running, but I was closing in with every day that passed. By the time I found the ship he'd taken out of Sydney, I was only a week behind him. I thought to overtake him, and got on a flight to Los Angeles, but when I arrived, I learned that his ship had deviated from its course. They went to Auckland, and then Santiago.

"I flew south, hoping to still catch him in Chile. Unfortunately, he was already crossing Peru into Columbia. I lost him again there, as he paid drug traffickers to smuggle him into the United States. It took four days of questioning every scumbag I could find before someone told me he would arrive in Laredo. Later that same day, in fact.

"So I hopped on another plane, and found myself in your fair country. That was three days ago, and now I've followed Surtr here. I know where he's holed up, but I can't take him on my own."

Nyk had been listening in silence, drinking beer almost as fast as the Irishman. I looked to him for his reaction to the story, knowing we'd need his help if we stood a chance against a jotunn. "Where do you think he's at? I'd like to surveil the place myself, get the lay of the land."

Padraig squinted his eyes as he looked at Nyk, then turned to me and raised his eyebrows. I knew he was asking if he could trust the bounty hunter, and I nodded. I would have trusted Nyk with my life. In fact, I had on more than one occasion. "Place called Natural Bridge Caverns. Popular spot, I gather."

I groaned, dropping my head to the bar. Of course the giant would be hiding in one of the largest tourist draws of the area. It made sense, considering what Padraig had said about the jotunn preferring caves. Thousands of people passed through the caves every month, but they stuck to the well-explored and safer areas. Miles and miles of unexplored or untraveled caves filled the area around the park. It could take weeks for an experienced spelunker to search them.

Nyk wasn't fazed by that, however. "I know a lady who can help," he said with a shrug. "She's spent the last fifteen years traveling through those caves, and she'll know the places to look for someone hiding out."

"I knew I could count on my man Dahlish to know the right people," Padraig said happily, slapping me on the back. "Let's call this lady up and head out there."

"Nope, she's asleep," Nyk said. I knew his tone, the one that said that's how it was, and you'd just have to accept it. "I'll call her at four a.m. when she starts work."

"I want to be there," Padraig insisted. "If anyone is going into those caves after Surtr, I'm going to be with them."

"Have any experience in caves?"

"No, but how hard can it be? I've been in tight spaces before."

Nyk only shook his head. "If you're not certified as an experienced caver, they won't even consider letting you join their expeditions. You'll have to wait for her to get back to me."

The Irishman threw up his hands in disgust. "It's been seven bloody months. I'm tired of waiting."

I put a hand on both their shoulders, taking on the role of peacemaker. "Nyk will get information for us as quickly as possible. There's no one else who could do the job as well as he does, Padraig. In the meantime, maybe you could fill me in on more details about what our talismans are capable of."

He drained his third beer, looking around the bar at Nox who still eyed us frequently as they tried to relax with two of the Nine sitting in the same room. "Aye, it's about time someone did. But not here. I'll come to your office tomorrow."

I was about to ask what time, but he just set his glass down, swiveled off the stool, and stomped out of the Den. Too late, I realized he hadn't paid or offered to pay for his own drinks. I guess that was a little bit more padding on the tab I had with Richard that never seemed to get smaller no matter how much I gave him after I collected on a good fee.

Nyk offered to pay for his three drinks, large glasses that had looked like child cups in his oversized hands. I waved him off, thanking him for coming to listen to the story and help out. He rose from his stool, then hesitated. "Jotnar are no joke, Jack. Whatever we end up facing in those caves, I want you to be ready for the worst. I'd never forgive myself if you ended up in a coma like the lady in India."

"I appreciate it, big guy. I'd rather not end up that way, myself." I smiled appreciatively, raising my still half full glass in his direction. "I promise I'll be as careful as I can. But we need to get a guy like that off the board before he kills more people."

He grunted, then pulled the door open and left the bar. As I nursed the rest of my drink, I realized the buzz of conversation was growing louder. Now that Padraig was gone, the Nox were feeling more comfortable and at ease. I grinned to myself, realizing that maybe they weren't as skittish of me as I'd always feared.

7

After I left the Den, I headed back to my office to catch up on administrative work. I had three cases I'd already been working on this week. Two of them were all but wrapped up, and I just needed to type up reports for my files and mail the bills out to my clients. The third was a standard divorce case. I'd followed a husband to not one mistress's house, but three. I had pictures of him entering and exiting each, with a few good shots of parting kisses. I called the wife and broke the news to her as gently as I could, sending the pictures to her email address while we talked.

She cried.

A lot.

I couldn't decide if they were sad tears, or happy ones because she'd get at least half of the man's small fortune in the divorce.

I was happy to have that behind me. The fees I got from such jobs were necessary to maintain my business, when so many cases like the one Ollie had pulled me into paid nothing at all. I enjoyed keeping people safe, but I still needed cash to keep the lights on. And I was pretty good at finding dirt when a husband or wife was cheating or trying to hide funds in advance of a divorce. Good enough that my old boss at a big private investigation firm still called me up to help when they had too many cases.

It was after nine by the time I wrapped all that up, and my eyes were burning from fatigue and cedar. February was always one of the worst months for pollen, and I had been severely allergic since my early twenties. If the talisman really did have healing powers, maybe I could get Padraig to show me how to fix my allergies. Then I could stop wanting to burn down every cedar tree I passed while driving around town.

I wasn't tired enough to head home and go to bed, though. In fact, I was still feeling keyed up from my date the previous night. That made me think of Karen, and I looked at the clock on my phone again. I had just enough time to get over to KRSA before the ten o'clock newscast. For the last several weeks, I'd made a habit of stopping in at least once a week to wish her luck.

The Wednesday night traffic was light, and I made good time. It was still fifteen minutes to ten when I parked in the small lot filled with cars, nabbing one of the few open spots. Where most office buildings were deserted at this time of night, it was the busiest part of the day for the television station staff.

It was a short elevator ride to the third floor, where I exited into a small reception area. The dragon lady sitting behind the desk still huffed with disapproval every time she saw me. Maybe it was because I'd been dressed down to easily mix with the homeless the first night she saw me. Or maybe she just thought someone like Karen Kilgraff should have higher standards that I could never hope to meet.

She did buzz me through without a word, though. I thanked her politely, as I always did, and went through the door. A left turn later, I was in a truncated hallway lined with half a dozen doors. Each door had one or two names on it, with

Karen's near the middle. She had a dressing room to herself as one of the featured anchors, the woman whose face was on almost every billboard for the station.

I knocked lightly, then pushed open the door without waiting for a response. Karen was a creature of habit, and I knew that she would be getting the final makeup touches at that moment. This time, though, I stopped in my tracks when I saw her standing in a rigid pose, facing a woman I'd never seen before. Karen's arms were crossed over her chest, and her brows were drawn together with frustration.

The other woman shifted her gaze to me, licking her lips when she saw me. "This must be the famous Jack Dahlish," she said, her voice almost a purr. "He's more handsome than you made him sound, Kare Bear." There was a vitality radiating from the woman that almost made me feel more alive just standing near her.

Karen gave me an apologetic look, then turned back to the strange woman. "Do not leave this room, Barbara. We're not done, and we're going to continue this discussion when I finish my work." She then grabbed my arm and led me out of the room.

In the hall, Karen closed the door of her room and then wrapped her arms around me. She was careful to keep her face away from my clothing, so her makeup didn't get smudged; it had to be heavily applied for the cameras. "Oh, Jack. You don't know how good it is to see you, but it's not a good night to visit."

"Is that the sister you told me about?"

"Yes. Barbara. She came by about an hour ago, and we're already fighting."

"Hey, it's what siblings do, right? I'm sure you both love each other quite a lot." She was silent but looked a little bit happier. "So, uh... Kare Bear?"

Karen groaned, almost leaning her head against my shoulder before remembering the makeup. "It's what she called me when we were kids. You know, Care Bears, those toys that were so popular back then. She knows I hated it after we moved on to high school, and she tosses it out now and then just to rile me up. It works."

A young man with a headset covering one ear hurried up from behind me. "Five minutes, Ms. Kilgraff." Then he continued down the hall, knocking on another door and poking his head in to repeat the time until broadcast.

Karen rubbed her hands on my chest, rising up to brush her lips lightly on mine. "I'd love to have you stay and talk after the broadcast, but..."

"But you have to deal with a younger sister, and the last thing you need is a clingy boyfriend around as a third wheel." I grinned to let her know I was joking. Mostly. I remembered how much my sister had annoyed me sometimes when we were growing up, but at the same time I would give almost anything to have her back to annoy me again. I very nearly had a month earlier.

"Thank you, Jack. I'll call you tomorrow. We need to plan another date."

"Sunday," I said with a wink. "I've already got a reservation at a place I know you'll love. Will you be my valentine?"

She laughed, reaching up to stroke my cheek in the way I loved so much. "I wouldn't want to spend it with anyone else."

I watched her hurry away, rushing to get onto the set and settled in her chair. Feeling eyes on me, I turned back to her door in time to see it closing. Barbara must have been peeking out, maybe listening to our conversation. I almost went back inside to ask her about that, but I decided to let Karen handle her own sister. I felt certain we'd be meeting again before she left town.

Back in my car, I dialed Ollie's number. It was late for a man who started work before eight every morning, but I knew he was often up until eleven or midnight. He answered after two rings, and I could hear the sound of a TV in the background.

"Jack."

"Hey, Ollie. I just wanted to call and see if you had any new information on the victim. Mariah said it was definitely the homeowner."

"Yes, we're sure of that. Time of death is hard to pin down, with the last known sighting two nights ago. But there was a food delivery last night, so we're hoping the driver can tell us who answered the door."

"Mariah mentioned that, too. Did you happen to get a look at the receipt? Or know where it was ordered from?"

"It was delivered from a barbecue joint, but they work with three different delivery services. I'm sure we'll know which one made the delivery by morning. The detectives were pulling the victim's credit card transactions, too, and the charge should pop up there soon."

"At least it'll give us some kind of lead on information. I've been hitting dead ends so far on my end."

There was a voice in the background, and Ollie's muffled response as he placed a hand over the phone. "Sandra wants to know when you're coming over, Jack. It's been too long since we had a cookout and chatted like normal people."

I thought about the forecast calling for frost early next week and shivered at the thought of sitting on a patio in that while watching steaks slowly cook over charcoal. "Tell Sandra that as soon as it gets back above fifty degrees, we're on. I'll drop everything for a night."

Ollie's grin was audible. "You know you're locked in now. She's not going to let you forget that promise."

After getting a promise from him to call me the next morning with any information discovered overnight, I turned my attention fully onto the roads. Traffic was light at that time of night, but there were still quite a few night owls out and about. I tried to imagine having a normal life again, going out to bars or clubs this late to hang out with friends. Those days were such a distant memory, and one that I reminisced on less and less often.

8

I was in my office a little after eight the next morning. I'd indulged myself with another breakfast at the café in La Villita and was feeling happily sated as I sat behind my desk. My big task for the day was to track down the new vampire clutch. I started by looking through police reports from the western side of town over the last six months. I noticed a small spike about four months earlier, and then the numbers began to fall. Say what you will about them, but vampires have a habit of making the areas around their lairs safer.

The biggest drop was in the North San Antonio Hills area. It was a smallish subdivision, with homes built twenty to thirty years ago on large two and three acre lots. I'd driven by it before, usually on my way to the newer and much more crowded Alamo Ranch area.

A few searches on real estate websites gave me a list of half a dozen homes sold in that area over the last year. I whistled as I looked at the prices, but then I remembered that the cost of the land alone would be growing by leaps and bounds with so much new construction out on the Far West Side. It was quickly becoming one of the hottest areas of town for people to move to, helped by several large corporate campuses near Sea World.

The neighborhood was also close to one of the parks I'd investigated a few months prior while searching for the abducted children. I'd detected the presence of vampires there, and I kept meaning to follow up on that since it was outside of the territories where I usually found such essences. I guess I'd finally gotten the kick in the butt I needed to get that done.

I was pushing my arms into my coat when my phone started to vibrate on the desk. I stepped over and picked it up, pressing the button to accept the call.

"Good morning, Ollie. Find anything good?"

"We've got another one, Jack." His voice was dour. "In Castle Hills, this time. You need to get out here." He gave me the address, and I wrote it down in the little notebook I carried with me at all times.

Fifteen minutes later, after breaking a few traffic laws, I pulled to the curb several houses away from where the police cars were huddled. The crime lab had two SUVs at the scene this time, and I could see a couple of people in polyester jackets with yellow SAPD lettering on the back walking the lawn carefully with their eyes on the ground.

I didn't know the cop standing outside of the yellow tape this time, but when I told him I was there to see Ollie he announced me over the radio and got quick approval to wave me through. The concrete walkway to the door was short here, perhaps ten feet from the sidewalk to the front door. I hoped the homeowners got a larger back yard in compensation for such small front yards.

The door opened when I was halfway there, and Anne Bishop stepped through it. She stood in the doorway, scowling at me as I approached. I'll admit, she was pretty intimidating for a woman who didn't even come up to my chin. "You better be as good as Sergeant Williams says you are," she said, poking a finger in my chest. "No one deserves to end up like this."

"I promise I'm doing everything I can to stop it, Annie."

She scowled harder. I knew she didn't like it when I called her Annie, and maybe that was part of the reason I kept doing it. Her disapproval was one of the few emotions I seemed able to elicit. Finally, she moved aside so I could squeeze past into the house.

Ollie was standing outside a bedroom down a short hallway off the main room. He waved me over as soon as he saw me and disappeared inside. I took a look around the large living room, noting the sparse furniture and lack of pictures on the walls. Entering the bedroom, I saw the same barren decorating style of a bachelor. There was a large dresser, a queen-sized bed, and little else.

Well, except for the husk of a corpse laying on the bed. The body was in the exact center of the mattress with the covers pulled up to his chest, and almost looked as if he had been sleeping when he died. Mariah Mathis was hunched over the bed, looking up to meet my eyes when I entered the room. I nodded in greeting.

"This one is almost exactly the same," Ollie said. "We're fairly certain this is Martin Ogelvy, forty-eight, bachelor. Lived in this house the last two years, and neighbors say they saw his car pull into the garage yesterday after work."

"Less than eighteen hours this time," I mused, getting as close to the bed as I was allowed while the forensics team was still working.

Ollie tapped me on the shoulder, jerking his head for me to follow. We left the room, walking back down the hallway and through the living room into a tidy kitchen. I caught the faint odor of coffee and looked to see a full cup underneath the spout of an automatic coffee machine. Mr. Ogelvy must have been a creature of habit, with the timer set for each morning.

I turned my attention to where Ollie was standing and saw a row of magnets on the fridge. Each of them was holding something to the metal surface. There were a few pictures that I assumed were the victim before he was drained and became a shriveled mummy. One postcard from San Diego, but I couldn't turn it over to see who it was from. And next to it was a receipt for food delivery. Peering closely, I could see it was for the previous evening, 7:34 pm to be exact.

"Well, that's an odd coincidence." I looked over the items listed on the receipt.

Ollie grunted. "Too much of one. The detectives are already running down the lead, talking with the restaurant owner to find out which delivery services he uses."

"Is it just me, or is this a lot of food for one person?" There was an order of mongolian beef, another order of cashew shrimp, six crab rangoons, and two iced teas. "I think our Mr. Ogelvy had a guest last night."

"Check the fridge."

Using the hem of my coat, I pulled the door open to look inside. Along with a few half gallons of milk, some sandwich fixings, and a jug of orange juice, there were two styrofoam containers. I looked to Ollie with raised eyebrows.

"About half of the food eaten from both," he said in answer to my silent question. "We've got uniforms knocking on doors to see if anyone happened to notice any visitors last night."

I closed the door and stood straight again, staring at the receipt. "The visitor could be a witness, but then I can't see a killer who was capable of doing this," motioning toward the bedroom, "letting someone survive the attack."

"At the very least, we can hope he or she saw something. Maybe a car driving down the street as they left, or someone on the sidewalk."

"Unless he or she was the killer."

Anne walked into the kitchen, ignoring me completely. "Sarge, the detective wants to see you."

I trailed behind as they walked out of the house, glancing through the rooms we passed. There wasn't anything that struck me as providing a link between the two victims. The first was a man in his seventies, retired and keeping himself busy around the house. The second wasn't even fifty, working hard, and living a quiet life from everything I could see.

The morning sunlight blinded me as I stepped out of the much dimmer house, and I had to blink for a few seconds until my eyes adjusted. When they did, I saw a gaunt man only a few feet away looking at me with an amused half smile. "Mr. Dahlish, I see you have joined us on this case."

"Detective Cavanaugh," I said in greeting. "I thought you worked missing persons cases?" The last time I'd seen him had been while I was searching for the abducted kids. He had even broken into my office to surprise me and find out what leads I had after providing some information for Ollie to pass along.

"I work whichever case the mayor tells me to work," he responded. I snorted, thinking of rumors I'd heard that there was a special unit set up inside the SAPD. Ollie had talked about them a few times, complaining as most cops did about detectives who were outside the chain of command. They answered only to the mayor's office, working the cases that Her Honor wanted solved before the media started talking about them too much.

"Well, this is a fun one," I said with a grin. I turned to go back into the house, knowing I wouldn't get anything from the detective that he didn't want me to know. Once inside, I took a deep breath and opened my senses. The interior of the house was almost devoid of any Nox essences aside from the vampire tracks left by Mariah.

And yet there was a faint trace of pink color around everything I looked at. As if whatever left it behind had been in the house long enough to stake a claim on the space. I could smell peaches, freshly harvested and on the cusp of ripeness. And I could feel myself growing sleepy as my eyes drifted closed.

"Hey!" A sharp poke in my side jerked me awake, and I turned to see Annie scowling at me. "No napping on the job, Dahlish. Late night with the lady friend?"

"No, actually. I only saw her for a few minutes last night." I rubbed my fingers over my eyes, trying to figure out why this Nox essence kept putting me to sleep. Defense mechanism, or maybe an attack method? I certainly hoped that the victims had been put to sleep and never felt whatever killed them.

"Detective Cavanaugh wants you out," she said, her voice a bit softer than usual. "Forensics needs the house."

I nodded and followed her back to the yard. There was no sign of Cavanaugh, which confused me. I'd only been inside for a couple of minutes.

"He left twenty minutes ago," Ollie said when I asked, looking at me with concern. "Bishop waited a while before dragging you out, to make sure you had time to look everything over. Are you alright, Jack?"

"Yeah. Yeah, I'm fine. Just got lost in my work, I guess." I waved as I walked back to my car, pulling my phone out of my pocket to check the time as I slid behind the wheel. It had been more than an hour and a half since I arrived, twice as long as I would have thought. What kind of Nox could put me out like that? There were some that could put you to sleep, but they would never leave behind a body like the two I'd seen. They were more likely to rob you blind and let you wake up to find everything of value gone.

A knock on the passenger window made me jump, and I pressed the button to lower the window. The cold air rushed into the car as my visitor bent to look at me. "Mariah, how's it looking in there? Do you think it could be the new clutch?"

She shrugged, leaning her arms on the top of the car. "I asked around last night, and no one in the family has been in contact with the west side arrivals. Uriah has been putting out feelers, but either no one has seen them or they're ignoring his attempts at contact."

"I did some research this morning. I'm thinking they're probably in the North San Antonio Hills area."

"And you're going to go driving around to see if you can find them?" She smiled and shook her head. "Be careful, Jack. Families don't like unexpected visitors, and especially ones with your kind of jewelry."

"I'll be discrete."

"Hey, the reason I came over. Like the last one, this corpse was shriveled down to almost nothing. Everywhere except the tongue. For some reason, that is swollen inside the mouth. I don't know if that helps you at all, but I thought you might want to know."

"Thanks for telling me," I said gratefully. She pushed off the car and walked toward one of the SUVs, where another crime lab tech was loading gear into the back of the vehicle. It felt good to know that I'd earned enough trust for her to share information freely.

Shivering from the cold breeze, I closed the window and cranked up the heat as I started the car. It would be a short drive to the Far West side of town, but long enough to get warm again.

9

I decided that the best place to start was in the park where I'd first detected the new vampire family. It was just outside Loop 1604, which had been the "outer loop" for decades until the city expanded beyond it over the last twenty years. The park was deserted when I arrived, all the kids in school on a February Thursday, and any joggers who might have used the trail at work by now.

The soccer field was still set up, and I stood on the edges of it as I opened my senses. The air was filled with the black streaks of vampire essence, and my nose was clogged with the smells of wet dirt and putrefying flesh. It was stronger than my last visit, fresher. As if members of the clutch visited the park most days.

I was about to close myself off when I got a hint of musky smell. Instantly, the back of my tongue was picking up a foul taste and I almost gagged as I shut off my access to the supernatural world. It was the leftover essence of the lamia I had tracked down, still lingering months later. It amazed me how strong she must have been to leave behind traces after so long. Not for the first time, I wondered how many years she had wandered around killing children and replenishing her strength.

But that case was over, and I had a new killer to track down before more people died. The vampire essence had been strongest around the soccer field, and streaks of it went back and forth to the parking lot. I wondered if perhaps the children of the family were on the team that practiced in the park.

A quick Google search on my phone found a website for the youth league. It listed the eight teams, and gave the names of the coaches, but didn't reveal any of the kid's names. I guess they had to be wary of predators who might latch onto the kids at games. One thing I did learn was that the next practice session was scheduled for Friday afternoon. I thought about waiting a day and coming back to find the vampires, but after two kills in two nights I couldn't just sit back and risk a third victim due to inaction.

The drive to the North San Antonio Hills neighborhood was short, especially after I got past the stacked-up traffic on the main street outside the park. It was almost noon when I turned onto the road that took me past houses on large lots. Some were a little worn, but most looked nice and respectable. A few looked magnificent, like the kind of home I would never be able to afford.

One of them stood out to me instantly. The property was at least three acres, and there was a high fence surrounding it. The black steel bars were no more than six inches apart, narrow enough to prevent anyone pushing through them. The driveway was blocked by a gate, and as I drove slowly past I could see three different cameras pointed at the spot where someone would stop to press the intercom button and announce themselves. That was a lot of security for a house in a safe part of town, and it looked newer than the home itself.

The house was beautiful, a two-story building faced with large white stones and rust red trim. The roof was covered in Spanish tiles, almost making it look like a Mediterranean villa transplanted to the middle of Texas. The windows I'd been able to see were darkly tinted, but expansive enough to make the interior feel open and airy.

Unfortunately, this wasn't the kind of neighborhood where I could park on the street and watch the house for any comings and goings. The roads here were narrow, and parking on them would draw attention. I drove past the house at least four times over the next hour, hoping to see a car in the drive or even a person standing outside in the large yard. But I saw nothing.

Exiting the neighborhood, I continued down 1604 until I found a place to stop and have lunch. I got a burger and fries at a Texas institution, the kind of restaurant I craved at least a couple of times a month. While I ate, I pulled up satellite maps of the neighborhood. Looking down on the property from above, I could see that there were at least three outbuildings behind the house. Loads of trees on the property that would shield any activity from view of the neighbors, too. It was exactly the kind of place I'd want to live if I were a vampire.

For a brief moment, I considered buying a drone and flying it over the neighborhood to get a view on the house. That would be breaking several laws, though, and would start things off in a bad way if the clutch discovered the surveillance. I had the name and phone number of the realtor who'd last sold the house, nine months earlier, but I didn't think he'd give me any information on the buyers. Privacy laws were such a nuisance for an investigator.

I was resigning myself to an afternoon of driving through the neighborhood hoping to spot something when my phone pinged with a text message. It was from Karen. *Sorry about last night. Dinner to make up for it?* Grinning, I quickly typed a reply to accept. We'd meet at 6:30, between her newscasts.

Moments after sending my reply, my phone pinged again. This time it was Nyk, telling me that his friend was in the caves and searching for any spots large enough for someone to hide. He'd warned her to be cautious, and not confront anyone she might come across. I'd almost forgotten about the jotunn after the second victim of my other case was discovered that morning.

I called Padraig's number, listening to it ring until finally a generic voicemail message played. After the beep, I told him about Nyk's message, and asked if he might want to help me out on my case while we were waiting. I hoped I would hear back from him soon. Maybe someone with more experience and knowledge would know of a way to track vampires.

After my lunch, I drove back to the neighborhood in the hopes of seeing movement at the compound that would either confirm or deny my idea that it was the lair of the new clutch. At the turn into the neighborhood, I was met by a police car. Two officers were standing beside it, and one of them stepped forward to hold up a hand and bring me to a stop.

He leaned over as I rolled down the window, his eyes searching the interior of my car. "Good afternoon, sir. Do you live in this neighborhood?"

Uh oh. "No, officer. I'm just driving around out here. Been thinking about buying a house in this area, so I wanted to see what might be on the market."

"Well, we've had reports of someone driving slowly through this neighborhood today. Someone in a car that looks a lot like

72

yours, actually. Several residents are afraid it might be burglars casing the area, and they asked us to check it out."

"Oh, wow. I can imagine how something like that can be scary. This is my first time driving through this section, though. It sounds like maybe it's not the safest area to move to." I gave a nervous laugh, feeling my hands starting to sweat.

The cop eyed me for several seconds. "You might want to come back another day."

"Sure, that sounds like a plan. I know my realtor could do the research for me, but I'm a bit of a control freak sometimes."

He patted the roof of my car a couple of times, stepping aside as I backed onto the access road for the highway. I waved as I pulled away, but the cops only watched me with terse expressions. I had to breathe a sigh of relief as I drove away, and also cursed under my breath. Of course a vampire family would already have contacts in the local police force. They must have caught me on their security cameras, and called it in.

I was frustrated as I drove, stymied in my search for the new clutch. And now they probably knew I was looking for them. The only thing I could think to do was wait until the next day and show up at the soccer practice. Trying to find them amidst a crowd would be difficult, but much easier than hoping to see someone drive away from a house and following them.

Another ping from my phone interrupted thoughts of what else I could do that afternoon, and I looked to see a message from Mariah. She wanted me to meet her at the crime lab building. I hoped that meant she had discovered something that could help my search.

When I arrived, I was surprised to see Ollie and Mariah sitting at one of the round tables shaded by large umbrellas outside the building. Annie was sitting with them but had her normal serious expression despite their laughter.

"What's up?" I asked, joining them on the concrete bench that surrounded the table.

"I found something in the latest victim, and I thought you should know." She reached into a pocket of the lab coat she was wearing, pulling out an item wrapped in a handkerchief. "This is still evidence, so no touching." Setting the white cloth gingerly on the table, she slowly unwrapped it until we could all see what was inside.

"Is that some kind of stinger?" Ollie asked, leaning down to look at the inch-long item that looked more like a thorn from a cactus to me.

"Whatever it is, it was embedded in the victim's tongue. I'm thinking it's what caused that part of his body to still be swollen."

"That is disturbing," Annie said, her brown eyes looking over the top of her mirrored sunglasses. I saw interest in her gaze, a curiosity that her gruff exterior kept hidden.

"That's not all," Mariah said, pulling a small plastic bag from another pocket. "This came from the first victim, but not his tongue." She laid it on the table, almost identical to the thorny looking thing in the handkerchief.

"Where was it on the first victim?" I couldn't remember any swollen appendage on that body, though he had been wearing clothes unlike our second victim.

Mariah coughed into her fist. "It was, uh, buried in the penis."

Ollie and I both grunted, feeling the pain of something like that thorn embedding itself into such a sensitive organ. "Murder weapon?" he asked.

"That's a theory we're looking into," Mariah said, wrapping the items up so she could put them back in her pocket. She looked toward the building's doors, and I knew she wasn't supposed to be showing us any of this. "The first was run through a few scans this morning. There were traces of some kind of chemical compound inside the hollow core, but the mass spectrometer hasn't spit out the results on those yet."

"Can you let us know when it does?" I asked. This discovery was helping me cross off a few types of Nox from my mental suspect pool. Finding out exactly what was inside the object could rule out even more. Vampires were still in, since I didn't know exactly what the new clutch was like.

Mariah promised she would, then apologized and rushed into the building saying her break was over ten minutes ago. Ollie and I shared a look, and I could see Annie looking between us. She knew there was something going on that she wasn't being told, and I could see it making her angrier by the second.

"Did the detectives get anything from the food deliveries?" I asked, hoping to deflect any questions from her.

Ollie shook his head and sighed. "There is one delivery company shared by both restaurants, but they don't show any orders from the barbecue restaurant two nights ago. That doesn't rule out the same delivery person, since they often split time with multiple companies. Cavanaugh is working to find that out."

"Maybe we'll get lucky," I said as I stood up. "Let me know. I'm still working on a possible suspect from my direction, but it's taking longer than I'd hoped." I wanted to tell him about the cops who were guarding the neighborhood I'd been searching, but I couldn't go into the story with Annie there. I'd have to explain why I had been there in the first place.

Ollie waved as he got into his cruiser, and Annie glared at me for a few seconds before climbing into the passenger seat. Call me crazy, but I had a strange feeling that glaring was her version of smiling.

10

I spent the rest of the afternoon doing research in my office, looking for creatures that might kill using barbs or thorns. Even fangs, though I couldn't see two of those snapping off in consecutive victims. That sounded pretty painful, and I think a creature that inept would have stopped killing after the first.

A few types of Nox did get added to the bottom of my list of possibilities, but none of them grabbed me like the idea of the vampires. I was half convinced that the reason no one knew anything about this new family was because they'd gone bad and moved to my town to get away from whatever crimes they'd committed in their last home.

By five thirty, I was at home getting cleaned up for my dinner with Karen. I stared at myself in the mirror for half a minute, considering shaving off the scruff that covered my face. Deciding against it, I just splashed on a bit of cologne and got dressed in my best t-shirt and cleanest blue jeans. I grabbed my coat on the way out the door and headed north.

KRSA's studio was in a three-story building just north of Loop 410, a little east of the northcentral area. It was a concrete building, painted white at some time in the distant past, with thin window slots dotting the four sides. I headed up to the third floor and found the most comfortable of the chairs in the reception area to wait for Karen. Dragon lady pretended to ignore me, but I could feel her disapproval from the moment I walked off the elevator.

I hadn't been waiting long when the door opened, and I saw a flash of red behind the man pushing through. Karen was close on his heels, and I stood up to present the small bouquet of pink tulips I'd managed to find at a flower shop on the way. I'd hoped for roses, but they were already sold out with everything new reserved for Valentine's Day over the weekend.

Karen squealed happily as she took the flowers, leaning in to give me a tight hug. "Oh, Jack, thank you so much. You don't know how much I needed something like this after the day I've had."

"That's what I'm here for, to always make your day a little bit brighter."

"You definitely do," she said, giving me a quick kiss. Dragon lady cleared her throat loudly, disapproval at Karen's choice of companion. I only smiled and waved as we entered the elevator to go downstairs.

"Where are you taking me?" Karen asked. "I'm famished."

"In the mood for Cajun? I know a place that does the best gumbo and boudin, not far from here."

"Let's do it," she said with a smile, linking her arm through mine and leaning her head on my shoulder as we walked through the parking lot to my car. I held the door open for her, then hurried around to get out of the cold. Karen was sniffing the flowers and smiling serenely as we drove the short distance to the restaurant.

The place was packed with the dinner crowd, but we were able to get a booth in a quiet corner. "What made your day so rough?" I asked after we'd placed our drink orders. Karen had asked for a hurricane, the first time I'd ever known her to drink between newscasts.

"Barbara," she said simply. "I just don't know what to do with my sister, Jack. I thought she would grow out of her wild ways, but here she is thirty years old and just as uncontrollable as ever."

"I guess that means you were always the good sister," I said with a smile.

"It was hard not to be," Karen sighed. She reached over to interlace her fingers in mine and pulled my hand close. "Ever since we were kids, Barbara has been the one with no impulse control. Whatever she wants is all she can think about, and she will do anything to get it. She lied to our parents so often that they stopped believing a word she said before she was even a teenager."

"That must have been rough to deal with."

"More than you know. My family moved around a lot, and usually it was because of Barbara. Something she did that made us have to leave town one step ahead of the consequences."

The drinks arrived, and Karen took a large gulp of hers. I could see from her tight expression that she was feeling much more stress than she normally carried. We ordered quickly, both getting gumbo and a plate of soft-shelled crabs to share. Once the waiter left the table, I decided to see how much more she might share about her past.

"Do you have any other siblings?"

"No, it was just the two of us." Karen snorted a laugh. "My mom always used to say that once they had Barbara, they were too exhausted to think about having more children."

I had to chuckle at that. It was so similar to something my dad once said about my own sister, though she was never as wild as Karen's sister seemed to be. Jen, younger than me by five years, had been driven by curiosity more than impulsiveness. It was that trait that had ultimately brought her life to such a short and tragic end.

"What places did you live? Do you miss any of them?"

Karen smiled, looking up at me through long eyelashes as she sipped her drink. She knew I was digging for as much information as I could get. I got lucky, and she was in the mood to share a little of it.

"I do miss Des Moines. We lived there for about a year when I was in high school. The kids there accepted me quickly, and I made a few friends before we had to move again. I even kept in touch with a few of them through college."

"Des Moines? That doesn't sound like the most exciting of cities." I'd never been there, but I'd heard about it from people who had. They said it was a nice city, full of nice people, but there wasn't much to do to keep you entertained.

"That's exactly why we moved there. I think my parents were hoping that Barbara could stay out of trouble in a place like Iowa. It didn't last, though."

"Maybe a small town would have helped. One of those places where everyone knows everybody by name."

Karen shook her head, grimacing. "We tried that, too. That lasted almost two months, but then we had to go."

"What was she doing? Drugs or something?"

"Something." Karen wrapped my hand in both of hers, smiling at me. "I'm so sorry, Jack. Here we are trying to enjoy a nice dinner together, and I'm just going on and on about my crazy sister. How has your day been?"

While we ate our gumbo and crabs, I told her about the discovery of the second body. She was surprised, which worried me since Karen always seemed to know about newsworthy events as soon as they happened. Her sister must have been a major distraction if she'd missed the news of the second victim on the police radio she constantly listened to.

I told her about the barb or thorn that Mariah had found, and then had to tell her how I'd met Mariah the day before. It made me smile to hear a tinge of jealousy in her tone when she asked about the other woman. Just enough jealousy to let me know that she really liked me and didn't want to lose me.

"Could it have been the tip of a needle?" she asked speculatively. "Maybe the killer is injecting them with something."

"No," I said, waving a spoonful of gumbo in the air. "It was too large for a needle, and it was definitely some kind of organic material. I would say it was almost like a bone if it weren't so small."

She went quiet after that, chewing her food with her eyes on the table. I wanted to ask what she was thinking about, but decided it was best to let her tell me in her own time. It had to be something involving her sister. Maybe she was contemplating telling me what Barbara had done to make the family have to move around so often.

The waiter brought the check before she could speak, and she glanced at the slim rose gold watch around her wrist. "Oh, that hour went by quick."

"Time flies when you're having fun," I said as I handed my credit card over to the waiter.

She returned my smile, taking my hands again. "Thank you so much for listening, Jack. And for being patient with me. I know you were probably hoping for more from me after a month of dating."

"Karen, don't worry about that. I love being with you, and I expect nothing but your company. It'll happen when it's the right time." I was wondering what had brought this on. We never discussed intimacy, though I won't lie and say I hadn't thought about it. It's hard not to, when you're so close to someone you have feelings for.

Walking back to my car, Karen pulled me close and gave me a deep kiss. The kind of kiss that makes you forget the world around you and sweeps you up in the wave of emotions. It seemed to go on forever and was over far too soon.

"Wow," I whispered, holding her close and running a hand through her hair. "What was that for?"

"For being such a good man, Jack Dahlish. I don't know what I did to deserve you in my life, but I never want to let you go."

"I feel the same way, Karen." I lifted her chin with a finger, leaning in to kiss her again. We probably would have been there for half an hour if some impatient diner hadn't flashed his lights and honked his horn. Apparently, the parking lot was full, and he was waiting for us to leave so he could park.

Driving back to the station, Karen kept looking over at me. It reminded me of the first day we'd met. I'd met her at the KRSA building after the last broadcast and we'd gone out for a late dinner. She'd stared at me during the entire drive, as if drinking in every detail of my face. It had made me so nervous then, but now it gave me a warm glow of joy. It had been ten years since I'd thought about having a serious relationship, and now that I felt ready the perfect woman had fallen into my lap.

Karen was smiling as we pulled into the parking lot of her building, and I thought that maybe an hour with me had helped relieve some of the stress she'd been feeling. I pulled up close to the entrance, and then ran around the car to hold the door open for her. I got another magnificent kiss as a reward.

"I'm looking forward to Sunday," she whispered hoarsely, in a way that got my blood pumping.

"Me, too. It's going to be the best Valentine's Day ever."

She laughed, turning to look at the building as if making sure no one was watching before she kissed me again. I saw her smile droop and her face get tight, and I followed her gaze to see a brunette woman standing just inside. Her eyes were locked on me, a sardonic smile on her face. "Barbara," Karen said, and I thought I detected a trace of dread in her tone. "Thanks again, Jack."

I watched her walk toward the building, noting the short, sharp steps she took and the way she yanked the door open as if it were fighting her. Something about seeing her sister had made Karen angry, and I couldn't help wondering what it was. Maybe she'd open up more this weekend and tell me what was going on between them.

As I drove home, all thoughts of Barbara dissipated as I thought about those kisses. They were fantastic and promised more later on. Perhaps Karen was thinking that she was almost ready to move into the next phase of our relationship.

11

A fter a night of blissful dreams, I overslept my alarm. Or, more accurately, I turned it off and didn't want to get out of bed. Winter always makes me lethargic in the mornings, and it's my work ethic more than anything that keeps me from lazing about more often. I had nothing planned for my day until the afternoon soccer practice, so I couldn't think of a reason to get up.

It was half past nine by the time I dragged myself through the office door and plopped down in the chair behind my desk. The morning sun was streaming in behind me, and for the thousandth time I told myself that I needed to invest in window shades for the office.

One thing the light did do was illuminate the man sitting in one of the client chairs. I jumped in surprise, leaning forward in case I needed to exit my chair quickly. About the same time, I recognized the red hair and dark vest. "What the hell, Padraig?"

"Aye, Jack. What the hell, indeed? Why haven't I heard anything from your friend the bounty hunter?"

I relaxed in my chair, biting back a few curses I wanted to spout. "The woman checking the caves is still working on it," I told him. Nyk had sent me a text the previous evening, and another while I was lazing away in bed. "She's back in the caves today, checking out more branches of the subterranean system."

"She should have found Surtr by now," Padraig said. I noticed he was holding a peak cap in his hand, twisting it around in his impatience.

"There are miles of caves down there, Padraig. And it's not like walking down the street peeking through windows. It's slow going when you're crawling through tight tunnels and navigating shifting rocks." I thought that sounded really good, especially for someone whose entire caving experience consisted of casual strolling through tours of several caves in Texas.

"I know," he said begrudgingly. "I've just been after this jotunn for so long. My city is unprotected right now because I'm chasing after Surtr instead of doing my job." He sighed, standing and walking to the door. "Learn this lesson, Jack. Don't make impulsive oaths, no matter how well-meaning they may be."

"Wait," I called as he started to leave. "I could use help with another case I'm working, and maybe you could tell me some things I should know about the talisman. Like how to use it for more than just detecting Nox."

His fingers were twitching, his body seemingly straining to keep going through the door. "Not today, Jack. I'm not in a fit state to be teaching you anything good. After we take care of the jotunn, then I'll give ye a day or two of training."

I groaned in frustration as I heard the outer door close behind him. To be so close to another one of the Nine, a man who had so much knowledge that I hadn't even realized existed until the last few days, and not be able to talk with him about it was maddening. If the coin hanging on a thin silver chain around

86

my neck had abilities that could help me be better at my job, then I wanted to know how to use them.

I realized there was nothing holding me back from trying to figure it out on my own. Ollie hadn't contacted me about another victim, so at least it appeared that our body-draining killer was giving us an extra day to catch them. There were several hours to kill before I could hope to track my vampires at the park, so I shrugged out of my coat and found a comfortable spot where the sun's glare wasn't striking my eyes.

Then I concentrated, focusing all of my willpower on the talisman around my neck. This was much the same way that I opened my senses to the supernatural world it allowed me to see. Even as I had that thought, the room filled with faint essence trails. Many Nox had passed through my office over the years, and I brought some of it in with me after being around them for extended periods. I didn't even try to sort out the various essence threads.

I poured more of my willpower into the connection, opening my mind to the coin and its abilities. As quick as a lightning flash, the real world faded into an insubstantial haze and the Nox essences disappeared completely. I felt a cooling breeze blowing across my face, catching the scent of eucalyptus and salt water. It became so strong that I was almost disappointed when I turned and didn't see a beach with waves crashing to the shore.

Come closer, a voice whispered. It seemed to come from every direction, echoing through my head. *Come closer, and you will find the power you seek.*

I knew this voice. I'd heard it many times in the past when I opened myself to the talisman too often during a case or

strained too hard to find something that would lead me to whoever I was looking for. The tempting voice, almost seductive in
its deep tones, one that was commanding yet beseeching. I'd
almost followed it too far more than once, losing myself inside
whatever shadow world I looked into when I saw the Nox and
the trails left in their wake.

Jack Dahlish, come closer!

Well, that was new. The voice had never called me by name
before. I was worried for a second, but then the cooling breeze
seemed to blow that emotion away and I was only faintly curious. And being pulled toward something. The misty walls of
my office, and the desk I had been sitting behind, faded away
entirely. The world around me became darkness, but I could see
light ahead. A small pinprick, growing steadily as I moved closer
and closer. My legs weren't moving. In fact, I couldn't feel legs
or arms or any other part of my body. And yet I was moving
toward that light.

*Yes! Come to me. I will give you everything you desire. You
will know power like no other man ever has.*

I stopped, though I'm not sure how. Something about those
words made me feel anxious. Cautious. The breeze blew
stronger, trying to clear that hesitation from my mind. I resisted
as much as I could, telling myself that I needed to leave this
place. It felt good here, too good.

Come closer, and you will know peace.

Peace? That sounded good. It had been too long since I'd
known true peace. I still blamed myself for my sister's death.
Blamed myself for hundreds of deaths through the years, when
I arrived too late or acted too slowly to stop a killer. How many

Nox had I killed that could have been saved? That thought kept me up most nights. Couldn't they have been rehabilitated and restored to their friends and family? Some I turned over to the human justice system, when I could be sure that prisons could hold them, and they wouldn't do more harm in such places. But too often the only way to stop the attacks was to kill the Nox committing them. Or to kill the humans attacking innocent Nox who had done nothing wrong.

You are not to blame. You did not know that my power awaited you. That it could help you be better.

That's what I really wanted. To be better than I was, always. Why couldn't I have found the new vampire family yesterday, or two months earlier? In fact, if I had real strength and power, they would have come to me when they arrived, to let me know they were in my city. To truly protect the people of San Antonio, I needed to be something more than I was. The Nox didn't trust me, they were uncomfortable around me, but they didn't fear me. Perhaps they should.

Not far now, Jack Dahlish. Closer. Come closer.

The light filled most of my vision now, and I could make out a few details within. Blurry shapes that made me think of furniture within a room. Could this be a part of the shadow world inhabited by one of the more powerful Nox? I'd been to the pocket of it under the overpass, where the strigoi Selma waited for fools such as myself to feed her with our memories in exchange for information that was more frustrating than helpful. There had even been rumors that the gods inhabited spaces of their own, worlds they retreated to for decades at a time when they tired of the people on Earth.

This is not mine, but yours. It is where you belong, Jack Dahlish. The place your power awaits.

I felt a tug, something pulling me back. I tried to turn a head that didn't exist, to look behind me. The breeze became a zephyr as I did, pushing me forward and keeping me from looking back. I wanted what was in that room. I had to know what waited there. Didn't I?

Closer. Only a little closer.

I stopped moving again, even as the wind pushed against my back. My brain was yelling at me not to go any farther, that I had already come too far. It was telling me to turn away, to return to the world I belonged in. The wind died down to a breeze again, filling my nose with the smells of the ocean. And for a second, I forgot all my doubts. But only for a second.

Still you resist, Jack Dahlish. Very well. I release you but give you a gift to show what awaits.

Something flew out of the room, a ball of blue flame that slammed against my vision. The light began to shrink, faster and faster as I felt myself flying back along the path I'd just taken. I reached out, regretting my decision not to go all the way even as the walls of my office began to coalesce around me. It seemed only seconds before the trails of Nox essence appeared once more, and then faded away as the reality of my office solidified.

I opened my eyes, breathing hard in a desperate attempt to fill my lungs with air. I felt as if I'd been submerged in water for too long, struggling to breathe and break the surface. It took me several minutes to catch my breath and lose the panic that had flared through my body when I came back to myself. I looked around my office, noticing that something was different but unable to force my brain to connect dots that seemed so obvious. When I saw my phone sitting on the corner of the desk, I stared at it for a long while before I realized what I was seeing.

It was already past two in the afternoon. That was why my office had looked so different. The light of the sun had faded as it passed beyond my window and moved toward the far side of the building where it would eventually settle below the horizon. It was dimmer, but with a much more comfortable orange glow from outside the glass. I had lost four hours to whatever trance I'd fallen into.

A pair of bathrooms at the end of the hall were shared by all the offices on my floor; none of us had enough space to justify a restroom in our own areas. I stumbled into one, turning the tap to splash cold water across my face until I felt the grogginess begin to lift. I stared at my pale face in the mirror, the dark bristles of a week-old beard standing out starkly in contrast. I thought I might look better than bodies lying on cold slabs in the morgue, but only just.

Standing there, I tried to remember what had just happened. I felt like I had known what it was when I left my office, but it was fading quickly in the way that dreams often do. Had I just fallen asleep in my chair and suffered a midday nightmare? Surely that had to be it. I remembered a voice, beckoning and cajoling. There was a light, far in the distance but getting closer.

But that was all.

I couldn't remember what the voice might have said to me.

Shaking my head, I splashed a bit more water onto my face and then reached out to pull paper towels from the dispenser and wipe the water from my skin. I felt better, but still disjointed in the way I always did when I fell asleep during the day. I should have known better.

Walking back into my office, I grabbed my gray herringbone coat and shoved my arms into the sleeves. That's when I remembered Padraig's visit, and his impatience with the search of the caves. I'd have to check in with Nyk, to see if there were any updates yet from today's searches. But I could do that in the car. If I didn't get a move on, I was going to miss my one chance to track the new vampires in town.

12

"I haven't heard from her yet," Nyk said over the speakers of my car as I drove across town. "Not much reception when you're underground."

"Well, that makes sense. Sorry, my brain is running a little slow this afternoon. Fell asleep at my desk."

"It happens," Nyk said, but I could hear him smiling. He knew how much I hated the grogginess after waking from naps, having experienced my grumpiness when I dropped off during a surveillance with him a few years earlier. "I promise I'll call as soon as Sonia gets in contact."

After the call ended, my radio switched back on automatically. I was listening to the BBC News channel, catching up on the latest world news while I drove. There had been an earthquake in northern Germany that morning, low on the Richter scale but still responsible for a few dozen deaths and hundreds of millions in damages. On top of that, there was flooding in Norway as the arctic ice continued to melt. While Texas was colder than normal, a strange heat wave had been torturing Siberia.

The park was crowded when I arrived, and I had to drive down to a second lot far from the soccer field to find a space. Kids were still arriving, fresh from their days at school, but it looked as if most of the team was already on the field. They were wearing yellow jerseys with blue lettering and had at least a dozen small patches advertising the businesses that had donated to keep the youth league going.

Parents were strung out along both sidelines, most of them sitting in canvas chairs in small groups. They chatted with each other for the most part, turning to yell encouragement at the field every now and then as their young sons or daughters kicked the ball around. The kids themselves appeared to be around nine or ten. Most of them were just having fun being with their friends, and I wondered how many of them really cared about winning or losing.

As I got closer, walking through short brown grass that crunched under my feet, two men hurried onto the field. Both wore shirts that were similar to the kid's jerseys. One was carrying a bag that contained more soccer balls, and the other raised a whistle to his mouth to blow piercingly and call attention to him.

"Alright, kids. Time to start. Everyone line up for me, and we'll begin with some goal kicks."

The kids clamored laughingly as they pushed and shoved to get in line, each of them trying to be on the side closest to the coach so they could be among the first to kick the ball. I had to chuckle at their enthusiasm and lack of temporal awareness to realize they'd all get a chance at it. I wondered if I had ever been that impatient as a kid, and then remembered times I could still be that impatient now.

Several heads turned in my direction as I joined the groups of parents. Most turned away just as quickly, but a few lingered as if wondering who I was. This was the third week of official practices for the spring season, and they were used to seeing the same parents every time. I smiled and waved toward the field, and the rest of the eyes turned back to the field when they dismissed me as an absentee parent who finally deigned to show up and watch their kid at play. Or at least I hoped they did.

I found a seat on a low stone wall that circled the sign for the park and some empty dirt that would hold flowers in another month when the weather began to warm up. I was close enough to the field to be able to watch the row of kids kicking the ball, but far enough to take in all of the parents without having to turn my head too much.

Reaching up to touch my talisman, I took a deep breath and began to open my senses. The essences snapped into my vision instantly, much quicker and more vibrantly than they ever had before. *I need to take more naps*, I thought in surprise, putting it down to being in a groggy state that made my mind more yielding.

The air was filled with black trails, just as it had been on my last visit to the park, but these were darker and more recent. It felt as if the Nox that left them had stood before me only seconds earlier. I tried looking at the parents lining both sides of the field, but it was hard to see them through all black streaks filling my vision. One of the downsides of seeing essence in a place so oft visited by Nox.

As if my thought had willed it, the essence trails dissipated and faded away. Almost as if they were blown away in a breeze, though the cold afternoon air around me was calm. Now I could see the people around the field clearly, and I began to look over them to see if any sported features that would tell me they were vampires. Most of the parents wore thick winter coats, with beanies or hoods covering their heads. Half of them were facing away from me, as well, making it even more difficult to see features.

The kids, however, were clearly visible. I couldn't help but look at their laughing faces as they kicked balls into the net while one coach acted as goalie and tried to block them half-heartedly. It amazed me to see a nimbus of light around the kids, as if their innocence were a beacon to the world.

Well, around most of them. Two of the kids, in the middle of the pack, didn't have a glow around them. In fact, they seemed to be almost shrouded in darkness.

I rose and walked a few steps closer to the field to get a better look at those children. Their faces were turned away as they laughed and talked to others in the line. When one of them did turn to look in my direction, I gasped and felt my body tense up. The boy's face was covered in sicky pale skin that almost looked as if it had melted onto his skull. The thick head of hair I had seen earlier was gone, the skin stretched tight with not a hair to be seen covering it. His ears drooped low, with points on the top in contrast to earlobes that dangled below his chin.

Gulping back the bile that rose in my throat, I turned away from the field and walked to the parking lot. There was a port-a-potty there, and I ducked inside to gather myself. I had never seen a Nox's true face so clearly and vividly before. It had always been like seeing a face behind a veil, such as you'd see on widows in old movies or television shows. The child's true appearance had been so sharp and real that I almost found it impossible to believe every parent in the park wasn't screaming in horror at the sight of it.

The stale urine smell in the port-a-potty drove me out after half a minute, and I stood there breathing in fresh air. I kept my face turned away from the soccer field, afraid of what I might see if I looked again. That's why I was surprised by the sound of someone clearing their throat.

"I'm done with it," I said, thinking it was someone waiting for the portable bathroom.

"Done with what, Mr. Dahlish?" The voice was hoarse, much like a two pack a day smoker would sound after a few decades. But there was still a bit of a sultry tone left underneath it. I turned to see a woman standing with her arms crossed protectively over her chest, looking at me with her mouth turned down disapprovingly.

"I'm sorry, do we know each other?"

"I know of you," she said, raising an eyebrow. "And I'd like to know why you thought it proper to come gape at my children in such a fashion."

I felt horrified, but relieved at the same time. This woman must be one of the vampires, and I was grateful to be seeing her human mask. I'll admit that for a while I was afraid that something had broken inside my head and I'd be seeing Nox for what they truly were all the time now. "I apologize, Mrs...?"

"Ms. Stefania Uribe." She stared at me, still frowning. "You haven't explained yourself, Mr. Dahlish."

I looked around, making sure that none of the other parents were close enough to overhear us talking. Reassured, I motioned for her to join me and walked away from the toilet in case someone else decided they needed it. Once we were a few steps away, we stopped in a place where we could see the kids on the field.

"The truth is, I was looking for you." I reached up to scratch the back of my neck, something I do when I'm feeling embarrassed. "I assume you're part of the new family in town."

She smirked, her eyes focused on the field. "There are a lot of new families in town, Mr. Dahlish."

"Yeah, but not the kind that get accused of sucking blood and raising the dead." I really hoped she was a vampire and not just a woman who happened to have met me somewhere. I should really have checked her out using the talisman, but I was afraid of what I'd see and how I'd scream like a little girl with her so close to me.

"The Uribe family has been in town for four months. It took you longer than I'd expected to track us down."

Phew. "I got a little sidetracked, but I'm here now. You know there are two other families in San Antonio?"

She snorted, looking at me with dark eyes. "The Harrisons and the Van Owens, yes. They don't concern me, as long as they stay out of our territory."

The way she was talking finally clicked. "You're the head of the family. The matriarch."

That earned me another smirk. "Indeed I am. We are a small family, though. There are only seven of us, including my son and daughter." She pointed toward the field, where the kids were now taking turns trying to block balls the coach gently kicked toward the net. I looked around at the parents, wondering if all of the family were present in the park. It would explain the thickness of the essence they left behind.

"Why now, Mr. Dahlish?"

"Hmm?"

"You said you were looking for us. Why now? I saw you here two months ago, and you seemed to have no interest in us then."

The time I'd been at the park investigating the scene of one of the child abductions. I had been looking for the lamia's trail then, noting the essence of vampires but relegating them to my very long to-do list. "There have been a couple of people killed recently, their bodies left drained."

"And you naturally assume the vampires had to be responsible. Did you go to Uriah or Emily, and ask them if they had done it?"

"There's more to it." I told her about the state of the bodies, the shrunken and shriveled husks left behind after they were killed. "I've been told that every vampire family has a different way of killing, so I need to find out how yours feeds."

Stefania was quiet, her lips pursed as she thought about everything I'd told her. Finally, she nodded. "Come with me, Mr. Dahlish. I'll show you that we are nothing for you to be concerned about."

She turned on her heel, marching toward the parking lot. I wasn't sure how smart it was to follow the head of a vampire family that no one knew a thing about. She could be luring me somewhere to kill me and stop me from asking questions. Or to turn me, which was rare but always something you had to keep at the back of your mind when dealing with that type of Nox.

When I hurried to follow, she was already standing beside a Range Rover and holding the rear door open for me. I looked

at her for a moment, took a deep breath, and slid into the vehicle.

13

A man was already waiting behind the wheel, and he started the vehicle even as Stefania got into the passenger seat. Within seconds, we were pulling out of the park. I looked through the smoky tinted windows to see if anyone was watching us, but even her kids were paying no attention to the Range Rover as it drove away.

"My family came here from El Salvador. We are a new family, Mr. Dahlish. Until a year ago, we belonged to the Chavez family in San Salvador."

That was unexpected. I'd always thought that vampire families were together forever. But it made sense that occasionally a part of the group might disagree and want to split off on their own. Much like teenagers eager to get away from the home they'd grown up in, so they could make their own path through the world.

"Hernan Chavez was a brutal man, the kind of vampire that gives the rest of us a bad name. I was human until thirty-eight years ago, Mr. Dahlish. A teenager who fell in with the wrong crowd, went to the wrong party, and endured weeks of torture and drainings until they turned me just for the fun of watching me try to fight the process."

Even more unexpected. In my experience, feral vampires were the only ones who turned humans by draining all of their blood and then feeding them some of theirs. It was a painful process for both parties, but especially for the human. If not done properly, they could be reborn an abomination that had to live with searing pain every moment of their mercifully short lives. If there was an entire clutch in Central America doing such a thing, then that was a family that needed to be ended.

"After a few years, the joy of watching me hate what I'd become grew stale. Hernan found new ways to torture me, and I was forced to bear him two children. Boys, who he took away from me and raised to be just as hateful and vile as he was." She reached up to rub at her eyes, turning to look through the window beside her. "Eventually, he had *them* torture me, as well. Do you know the kind of hunger one of our kind feels when we are kept from feeding for years at a time? I assure you, Mr. Dahlish, it is enough to drive most of us insane."

Something I knew all too well. One of the cases I'd had to handle in my early years wearing the talisman had been a feral vampire. A man who'd been trapped underground by a cave-in more than twenty years earlier, assumed dead after several days when the searchers gave up on finding him. New construction in the area had exposed his presumed grave, releasing the crazed creature. He fed on the four constructions workers who found him, leaving their drained bodies behind before escaping to search for more victims.

"I persevered, and in fact I only grew stronger as they tried to break me down. Even when Hernan had my own sons breed with me, I would not give him the satisfaction of losing my sanity. I bore my sons' children, and that was when I found the method of my escape.

"One of the guards on my door was a surprisingly gentle man, horrified by the things being done to me. He snuck into the room during the day, while I was left alone, and spoke to me. He kept me grounded, kept me strong." She reached over to stroke the driver's arm, and I knew he had been the man guarding her door. "With his help, I gathered everything I needed. It took months, but finally I was ready to take my revenge on the family that had given me nothing but hatred and pain."

Suddenly, I remembered a story I'd heard on BBC Radio a few years earlier. Something that had happened in Central America, beyond Mexico, where most Americans rarely paid attention to anything that wasn't drugs or brutal dictators.

"When Hernan visited me again, I let him have his way with me. I let him open my veins and coax out blood that was turning to sludge after too long without feeding. I let him force himself into me and lay there until I knew he was focused on his own pleasure. That's when I pulled the hidden blade from my mattress, and I plunged it through his foul heart before he even knew it was coming."

She twisted in her seat, looking back at me with angry eyes. "Have you ever killed a vampire, Mr. Dahlish?"

"Once," I said quietly.

"It's a difficult thing, is it not? He fought me, even as his own blood drained from his body. Even as I drank every drop of it and felt myself becoming stronger with it. Finally, he stopped fighting. He knew I had won. And I chopped his head off to be sure he could never survive to come after me."

Stefania turned back to look through the windshield. We were getting closer to North San Antonio Hills, and I could see the sign for the neighborhood in the distance.

"My sons were next, the children I had been allowed to love for only minutes before they were taken away from me to become monsters. They rushed into my room, wondering why their father hadn't returned to them, and found his head staring at them with blank eyes. I think a part of me hoped they would be joyful in that moment, that they would show they had suffered under him as much as I had. Perhaps then I could have spared their lives and brought them with me.

"But it was not to be. They hissed at me, called *me* a monster, and attacked me with hatred in their eyes. I killed them, taking their blood into my body and absorbing their strength. I know it makes me a bad mother, but I enjoyed their deaths. Watching them scream with pain as they felt a small bit of everything they had done to me over the years.

"My protector joined me then, with a few others who felt as repulsed by Hernan's ways as he did. Together, we fought our way through the family compound until only a handful of the Chavez family remained to flee into the night. I rescued my youngest children and brought them with me. They will never know who their fathers were, and I will always love them no matter how they came to be."

The Range Rover slowed, turning into the neighborhood. I looked through the window to see another police cruiser sitting there with two cops leaning against it.

Stefania laughed. "One thing I did learn from my experience, always be sure that you are protected wherever you end up. A large portion of the cash I stole from Hernan's compound went to pay off the authorities here. Your police are more expensive than those in El Salvador, but they are just as willing to be bought when you offer the right amount. When we saw a car driving through our neighborhood on our cameras, we had to be sure it wasn't some remnant of the Chavez family that had managed to track us here."

"Is that why you haven't reached out to the Harrisons or Van Owens? Are you afraid one of them might be like the people who made you a vampire?"

"No, Mr. Dahlish. I have learned that such monsters are uncommon. I keep my distance from the other families because we value our privacy. I didn't come to San Antonio to become a powerful matriarch, pulling strings in my part of town and building a fortune. I came here because I knew I could find a place to live, a place where I could stop looking over my shoulder every minute of the day." She turned to smirk at me. "A place where a man would fight to protect me if the Chavez family tried to attack me."

The vehicle stopped again, facing the gated house I'd looked at the day before. The driver reached up to press a button on a remote clipped to the visor and we watched the gate slowly pull back until the Range Rover could roll forward again. The entire time, I was thinking how odd it was that Nox had decided to move to San Antonio for my protection. I wondered whether she was disappointed that I hadn't reached out sooner or pleased that I'd left them alone until now.

We drove around the house, turning off the main driveway onto a smaller one that circled around to the back where a long carriage house sat. There were four garage doors, each separated by at least three feet of stone facing. I was curious about what might be contained in such a large building, but the driver came to a stop before entering it. He and Stefania exited the vehicle, and I reached over to try and open my own door, finding it locked. It was soon opened by the driver, a man who looked imposing and massive as he stood there waiting for me to exit. He was easily half a head taller than me, with wide shoulders and biceps that were straining the seams of his nice suit.

Stefania was waiting as I slid out of the Range Rover, and she waved for me to follow as she turned and walked away from the house. We walked along a flagstone path in silence for a few minutes, passing between tall oak trees and approaching a couple of outbuildings that were situated in a L shape ahead. She paused before we rounded them.

"This is what I wanted to show you, Mr. Dahlish. The reason you don't have to worry about us being the killers you are searching for."

When we rounded the first building, which turned out to be a low barn, I was assaulted with the smell of manure. I'd been detecting it in the air since getting out of the vehicle, but it was almost unbearable once the buildings blocked the wind that had been blowing the stench away from us. A large pen filled the area, churned up dirt and mud with a couple dozen pigs wallowing or oinking as they snuffled around the feed troughs.

Two women wearing overalls were in the pen, shoving a large sow toward the far building where a small door was open. They were cursing and straining against the pig that easily weighed as much as both of them combined. And yet, the sow moved half a foot or so with each shove, unable to resist the unnatural strength behind those arms.

"So, you're pig farmers? I'm not sure what I'm supposed to get from this that drops you from my suspect list."

She motioned for me to follow again, leading me toward the second building and through a rough wooden door to the darkness within. Even before I stepped inside, I could hear the squeal of the sow, finally pushed through the small door from the pen.

I entered to find the pig kicking and squealing as its hind feet were wrapped in thick rope that descended from several large pulleys overhead. One of the women in overalls held the other end of the rope, straining as she pulled on it once the sow was tightly bound. The pig jerked and squealed louder as it was lifted from the ground to hang several feet in the air.

"This is where we get sustenance," Stefania said from behind me, her breath warm on my ear. "When I left El Salvador, I pledged that my family would never drink from humans again. I would never subject anyone to the torture I suffered, even if they volunteered for the so-called honor."

One of the women produced a large knife, the blade gleaming in the rays of sunlight that shone through chinks in the wooden roof of the building. It flashed as she whipped it through the air, and the sow was suddenly silent as the blade sliced through its throat.

That was when I noticed the funnel and glass jar that had been placed below where the sow was hanging. Blood poured from the wound, a few drops scattering across the dirt and hay covered floor but most falling into the funnel. It seemed to flow like a river, and before I realized it the glass jar was almost a quarter full.

"This is where we take our food," Stefania said, stepping around me and holding an arm toward the sow. "Whatever it is in human blood that nourishes our bodies, most of that can be found in the blood of pigs. We must drink more of it, but as you can see one of our animals is enough to sustain our family for a week."

The two women working around the pig ignored us as they ministered to the sow, making sure that every drop of blood was drained from the body and captured in the glass jar. Behind them, I could see an expensive setup of gleaming stainless steel. There was a refrigerator there, along with a warming oven that I thought must keep the blood at the right temperature for the vampires to enjoy.

"Okay," I said, then had to stop to lick my dry lips. "I never thought about the possibility of something like this before. Why don't more of the families do it?"

Stefania laughed, guiding me from the barn as the other women completed their work. "As you said, every family is different. What we take from blood is not the same as what another family might need. Some feast on the iron that flows through your veins, others only on the salt. Still others need the hemoglobin. All of it can be obtained from other sources, but it's never as filling or as sustaining as when it comes from one of you."

It made a strange kind of sense. After all, I knew that humans in different regions of the world had come to need different quantities of vitamins and minerals, depending on the evolution of their origins. Why not the same thing for vampires? It was a fascinating subject, and I would have to do more research on it. Sometime when I wasn't tracking a killer and apparently having to start over at square one.

"You're sure that none of your family could have decided the swine blood wasn't enough for them, and gone rogue to get their own food?"

"I assure you, Mr. Dahlish, none of my family would break our rules. We may be a new family, but we are closer than most. My word is law among the Uribe clutch. Isn't that right, Javier?"

That was the first time I noticed the driver had been trailing a dozen steps behind us. I turned to see him nod, his gaze direct and honest. I'd already figured my idea was a strike out, but that clinched it for me. Whatever they had done in El Salvador to escape Hernan Chavez, they were peaceable in San Antonio. Hells, they were probably providing the pig meat to the local boutique butcher shops to help keep small businesses alive. That alone made them pretty decent in my book.

We piled back into the Range Rover, and Javier began the trip back to the park. Stefania turned to look at me, her eyes imploring. "Do you see now, Mr. Dahlish, that we are nothing for you to worry about?"

"I do, Ms. Uribe. I'd appreciate it if you could reassure the other vampire families of that, though. The last thing I need is a war between all of you because they got twitchy when you wouldn't play nice."

She sniffed but smiled at me. "Very well. I will get in contact with Uriah Harrison and Emily Van Owen soon. Perhaps it will be good for us, as well, to not have to worry about the other families taking our silence the wrong way."

"They would probably be willing to help out if the Chavez family remnants did show up," I said. She pursed her lips in thought but didn't reply.

For the rest of the trip back to the park, my mind was churning and trying to figure out what to do next. Even though I'd started out thinking it was a low probability, I'd been increasingly certain the vampires were responsible. Especially with the victims being so near the border between this territory and that of the Van Owens family.

There was still the wraith idea, which did fit the corpse better. The vengeful spirits tended to stick to a tight area, though. Wandering wraiths were even more rare than wraiths themselves. And the thought of Lamashtu or some creature like her was unlikely due to the victims themselves. The demoness was said to target pregnant women and nursing children, so why would a Nox that myth could have been based on be killing single men in their middle age and later? I'd have to do some background checks, but I felt pretty confident that neither man even had children of their own.

Soccer practice was wrapping up as we returned to the parking lot. Javier got out and stood beside the hood of the Range Rover while Stefania and I walked toward the field. She smiled and waved at the two children who looked so much like her now that I was able to see their human faces. They waved back before continuing to laugh and play with their friends.

"I do hope you find this killer of yours, Mr. Dahlish. I wish no harm on any human, and it pains me that some of our kind would do such a thing."

I knew she meant Nox as a whole, and not just vampires. "Thank you, Ms. Uribe. I'm sorry I disturbed you during time with your children. I'm glad we finally got to meet, though."

"Yes, I'm glad of that, as well. And please, call me Stefania."

So, I found myself behind the wheel of my car, driving south back to my office, in the same place I'd been two days earlier. Only now I was one suspect down and looking at a list that didn't stir the imagination. I was feeling lower than I had in weeks, when the text message pinged on my phone.

14

It was from Karen, and that made me smile. The message itself when I unlocked the screen made my smile wider. *Feeling lonely. Come see me. Luigi's, now.*

I checked the time on my phone. It was almost five, so I was a little confused about why she'd want me to meet her at a restaurant ten minutes from the studio. But maybe she was taking a break from anchoring the five o'clock news, as she did a few days each month. I wasn't going to question it too much, since I wanted to see her just as badly as she wanted to see me.

Rush hour traffic slowed me down, turning a fifteen minute trip into almost twenty-five. Every time I started to get irritated, though, I reminded myself of how much worse the traffic was up the road in Austin, or out in Houston. I'd been through rush hour in both cities many times, and if you got to your destination in less an hour you considered yourself grateful. Especially if you were going across town.

Luigi's was a small Italian restaurant, tucked away in a small strip mall built several decades ago. It was off the main streets, and you almost had to know it was there to find it. Karen had been the first to take me there, in those early days after we met. The food had proven to be so good that I went back every few weeks, and often with Karen when she could get away for lunch or a late dinner.

I had a wide smile on my face as I walked through the door, looking around the small restaurant for wavy red hair that I knew so well. There were only a handful of occupied tables, and I didn't see Karen at any of them. I did see another familiar face, though. One that was leering as our eyes met, making my own smile melt like butter on a hot July afternoon. I walked over to the table at the rear of the room, standing there for several seconds.

"Barbara," I said tersely. "I'm guessing Karen didn't send that message."

"No, but I knew you wouldn't come if I asked you. Sit down, lover boy." She pushed the chair closest to her back, but I ignored it and sat across the table from her.

"What's this about? Why the trick to lure me here?"

"Jack, you're dating my sister," she said, as if that explained everything. "I want to know what kind of man you are, make sure you aren't going to break poor Karen's heart."

"I would never do anything to hurt Karen," I assured her, relaxing slightly. An overprotective sister I could deal with. At that moment, the waiter arrived to hand me a menu and recite the evening's specials. He was a man who had seen me with Karen a few times before, and I could tell from the way he looked at me and Barbara that he was wondering how much of a jackass I was. It didn't help that the sisters looked almost nothing alike.

Barbara didn't take her eyes off me the entire time. She ordered red wine and a scallop dish, while I went with water and chicken parmigiana. It felt wrong to order my favorite ravioli without Karen there.

As soon as the waiter walked away, she smiled at me and placed her chin in a delicate hand. "So, tell me about yourself. Do you have any family in town?"

"No, my parents and sister are gone," I said. There was no way I was going to share intimate details about them with someone I barely knew. Especially when I was still a little mad about the way she got me to meet her.

"Hmm, that's too bad. I hope you at least have some close friends. It's not good for a person to be alone."

"I have Karen," I reminded her. "There are a couple of other people I consider very close friends, too. Ollie is a cop with the SAPD, and we work together on cases now and then. He and his wife Sandra have become some of my best friends in town." I blinked, trying to figure out why I'd just shared all of that.

"A police officer, how exciting. I bet he could tell me some fantastic stories about you."

The drinks arrived, just in time since my mouth was growing dry. I gulped down some of the water, licking my lips to moisten them. "There are a few, but they're not really that exciting."

"Oh, I don't know." She winked at me over her wine. "I imagine you see all kinds of wonderful things in your job as an investigator. What do you investigate the most?"

"Whatever comes through the door," I said with a false laugh. It was the standard answer I gave when people asked the question, to avoid any follow ups. Then I felt my mouth open to add, "A lot of divorce cases, but mostly murder, assault, and missing people. Anything that might be tied to them."

"Them?" Her eyebrows went up, along with the corners of her lips.

I had to struggle not to talk about the Nox, while trying to figure out why I was being so talkative. I remembered feeling much the same way the first few times I met Karen, but I'd been happy to share everything with her. Now, with Barbara, it felt more like an unwilling admission after hours of relentless questioning. I had to stop it somehow. "It's your turn, Barbara. Do you and Karen have any other siblings?"

Her amber eyes flashed with disappointment, but she leaned in to answer my question. "It's just the two of us, always has been. I like to think that my parents realized they couldn't do any better and they stopped after I was born."

At least that matched what Karen had told me, though the reasoning was different. "Where do you live now? What kind of work do you do?"

Barbara laughed, an unpleasantly grating sound coming from deep in her chest. "I move around a lot, Jack. I don't like to be in any one place too long. Welcomes are nice, but they seem to fade after a few weeks."

I noticed she avoided the question of work, but the food arrived before I could press it. The waiter smiled at her as he set down the scallop linguine, and then gave me a disappointed frown as he set down my plate.

"What are your intentions with my sister?"

I was surprised by the question, coming from nowhere after we'd been eating in silence for a minute. I hurriedly chewed the bite in my mouth before answering. "I love her, Barbara. I hope we're together for years to come."

"And will you ever propose, or just keep her as your side piece while you roam around doing whatever you want?"

The venom in the question stunned me. I had to wonder if she was speaking from her own personal experience, or if something like that had happened to Karen in the past and she never talked about it.

"She's the only one for me. I would never cheapen my feelings for her by getting involved with someone else while Karen is in my life."

"Never?" she asked.

I shook my head. "Never."

She looked at me speculatively after that, seeming to examine me while she was pondering deep thoughts. I was trying to decide how much of this I should talk to Karen about the next time I saw her when Barbara changed the subject.

"Tell me about this case you're working on. Kare Bear said there have been some murders, and you're helping the police to find out who did it."

"Something like that." Back into uncomfortable territory. I never really like talking about cases, especially the ones I was working on. I might discuss it with Karen or Ollie, even Richard every rare now and again, but it was hard to talk about it with an almost total stranger. "A couple of men were killed in their homes. We know roughly what time they were last seen alive, giving us a short window on the time of death. But the strange thing is that the bodies were shriveled up and dried out, as if they'd been sitting in the desert sun for a few months instead of in comfortably heated homes overnight."

There I go talking without thinking again. What the hell was going on with me tonight? I drained the rest of my water to force my mouth to stop talking, then looked around for the waiter and waved the empty glass.

"Absolutely fascinating. How do you think something like that happens?"

"I'm not sure yet, but I have a couple of theories. I ruled out vam..." My teeth clicked as I forced my jaw shut, and I felt my cheeks going red with embarrassment. The last thing I needed was my girlfriend's sister thinking I was some crazy loon. Being a source of strife in a family was a sure way to end a relationship quick.

The waiter saved me again, arriving with a pitcher of iced water to refill my glass. He asked if we had saved room for dessert, and I was quick to decline and ask for the check. I had to get out of there before I talked too much.

Barbara only smirked at me, her eyes seeming to convey a feeling of victory. I wasn't sure what contest she had been playing at, though. Hopefully, it just meant I had passed whatever test she had for the men who dated her sister.

The waiter arrived with the check, and I pulled out my wallet. Normally, I would plop down my credit card to pay for almost everything so I could reap the rewards of my cash back points. Tonight, I pulled out cash so I could get out of the restaurant quicker.

I felt something brush my leg, and my hand froze as I was counting out bills to cover the check and a tip. The feeling came again, longer this time as her foot seemed to caress my calf. When I looked up, Barbara only winked and ran her tongue over her red lips. This *had* to be a test, right? There was no way she would come on to her sister's boyfriend, after I'd just talked about my strong feelings for Karen.

Right?

The foot went higher, and I yelped as I shoved my chair back. She chuckled lowly as I stood up and dropped cash on the table without looking at how much I'd pulled out. "It was nice talking to you," I said as I turned and hurried out of the restaurant.

Sitting in my car, I rubbed a hand over my face trying to figure out why I had been so talkative. Maybe it was a Kilgraff family trait, some sort of charisma that made people open up and spill their thoughts. Why did Barbara trick me into meeting her that way in the first place? She could have just called and asked me to meet her, without pretending to be Karen.

My skin felt uncomfortable as I drove away, too tight on my body. It was kind of how my stomach always felt when I ate an entire pizza by myself, but across every part of my body. I shivered, thinking of the poor men left dead in their homes, then laughed at myself for equating my own strange feeling with the way they had been drained of blood and vitality.

I also felt incredibly tired, for some reason. Maybe it was the emotions that fought inside of me during the dinner, using up all the energy I'd had left after my unplanned nap earlier in the day. My idea of heading back to the office to start on more research was scratched as I yawned widely enough for my jaw to pop. Home and bed sounded much better to me in that moment.

15

When my eyes opened, sunlight was streaming through my bedroom window. That seemed wrong to me, but my brain was too groggy to put much thought into it. I rolled over, pulling the covers over my head, and groaned with the exhaustion I still felt. If someone had told me I'd fallen asleep two minutes earlier, I would have believed them instantly.

Then I heard the sound of a lawnmower. It took me a few seconds to connect the dots and start wondering who mowed their lawns on a cold February day. My eyes popped open again when I realized there was only one person on my street that obsessive. He was a young guy, in his late twenties, and swore up and down that mowing your yard year-round kept the grass healthy. And he did it every Saturday around ten a.m.

I fought my way out from under the covers, feeling panic rising in my chest as I reached out for my phone. It was laying on the bedside table instead of on the charging stand, which told me I'd been more exhausted than I realized when I got home. I tapped the screen and yelled with frustration when it didn't light up. The battery had gone dead while I was sleeping.

I slapped the phone into the charging cradle, swung my legs over the side of the mattress and stood up. I had to raise my arms in a groaning stretch before I could walk into the kitchen and look at the clock over the stove. 10:17

"Ah, hells," I said as I rushed into my bathroom to shower and get dressed in mostly clean clothes. It was long past time to do laundry again, and I still hadn't done anything to get the plumbing fixed in the small room behind the kitchen that was supposed to hold a washer and dryer. The jeans were clean, though, and the shirt smelled fairly fresh thanks to my foresight of putting it on a hanger instead of dropping it into the basket of dirty clothes after wearing it last.

My phone had enough of a charge for me to power it back up, groaning as I saw half a dozen missed calls and a couple of voice mails. Two calls from Nyk, three calls and a message from Padraig, a call and voice mail from Karen. I listened to the voice mails first.

"Dahlish, if your friend can't get me any results by the end of the weekend, I'm going into those bloody caves on me own. Tell him to have his friend get off her arse and search faster!"

The Irishman was getting even more impatient, but I knew Nyk's contact was working as quickly as she safely could. I certainly didn't envy her having to crawl through those underground caverns and tight spaces trying to find the hiding place of a dangerous murderer. The fact that Nyk hadn't left a message when he called told me he didn't have anything to really report.

Karen's message played next. "Jack, I am so sorry. I just saw the message Barbara sent to you while I was out of my dressing room. Please tell me she didn't make a fool of herself. Call me."

Talking to Karen was number one on my priority list. With only three percent of my battery, though, I'd have to call her from the car. Learning my lesson from a previous case, I now kept two chargers there. I slipped into my herringbone coat, grabbed my keys, and opened the front door.

Ollie was just getting out of his patrol car, with Annie standing on the far side. She even looked a little concerned for a moment, until she saw me and her usual scowl erased any other expression.

"Jack!" Ollie hurried up the walkway. "I've been calling for hours, and it keeps going straight to voice mail. What's going on?"

I looked down at my phone, noticing that the last missed call had been around midnight. The battery must have died after that and it didn't report the calls that came in while it was powered off. "I didn't put it on the charger," I explained, holding up the phone.

"Well, I'm glad it was something small." He tucked his thumbs behind the belt carrying loads of gear around his waist. "There was another one. This one was at an apartment complex, and the body was outside on the patio. If he hadn't lived on the first floor where a neighbor could spot the body, I don't know how long it might have been before we knew about it."

"This day just keeps getting better," I muttered. "Where was it this time?"

"The complex is about half a mile west of 281, almost smack dab in the middle of 410 and 1604."

I knew the area well. It was the part of town I'd lived in during my last year of college and when I started my first real job that I'd hoped would turn into a career. There were quite a few apartment complexes around there, though.

"Come in and give me the details. I'll make coffee." I held the door open for Ollie, and then waved for Annie to join us. She hesitated for a few seconds, but then walked slowly down the walk and pushed past me. She looked around at my home curiously.

"Doing a little work on the place?" Her glance was appraising, but I was pleased to see approval in her eyes as she took in my small home.

"Too little," I said. "I started on the floors over a month ago, and still haven't finished them."

Ollie and Annie followed me into the kitchen, taking the two chairs around a small table I bought at a garage sale years ago and rarely used. I spent some time filling the coffee maker with water and pouring grounds into the filter cup. Once I hit the button to start it brewing, I leaned against the counter and waved for Ollie to start.

"The body was discovered a little after six this morning. A woman going to her car to drive to work saw the shriveled corpse sitting in a chair on the patio. She said she thought it was some kind of creepy Halloween decoration at first, but when she got closer, it looked too real. Thankfully, she decided to call 911 just in case.

"First unit on the scene had to crawl over the railing to get close and confirm it was a real body. This one was a little different, Jack. It was still... wet, I guess you'd call it. Juicy? Like whatever is killing them didn't completely finish the process this time."

"Yeah, this one looked more like a raisin than a mummy." Annie almost smiled as she spoke, before the scowl returned. I had to hide a grin behind my hand, thinking that she was becoming comfortable enough around me to show more of her true self.

"That's a disturbing image," I said. "Do we know if there was a food delivery this time, too?"

Ollie shook his head. "No receipts for it, at least. Detective Cavanaugh did finally track down the delivery drivers for the previous victims. Different people, one man and one woman. No connection between them, as far as we can tell, so it's being considered unrelated to the deaths."

"How about an identification?"

"That we do have." Ollie pulled his notebook out of a chest pocket, flipping through pages filled with his neatly scrawled handwriting. "Vic's name is Gerald Jones, age thirty-nine. Lives alone as far as we can tell, divorced several years back and his ex-wife moved out of state. Cavanaugh is tracking her down, just to rule her out completely."

I poured coffee into three cups as I ran that name through my head. There was something about it that was strikingly familiar, but I couldn't make the memory stand still so I could catch it. I already knew Ollie liked his coffee black and bitter, but I pulled out a few packets of sugar for Annie and asked if she needed milk. I was amused to learn she liked it the same way I did – one sugar packet and just a splash of milk to cut the bitterness.

"Wait a second. Gerald is shortened to Jerry a lot, right? So this guy could have called himself Jerry Jones?"

Ollie shrugged. "I suppose so, why?"

"Pretty sure he wasn't the owner of the Cowboys, Dahlish." Annie even grinned as she said it.

"No, but I know someone with that name. I made a joke about it once, and asked him why he paid the running back so much on the new contract." I felt my legs go wobbly as I realized that this latest victim could be someone I knew. Not only that, someone I'd just seen the day before. "Do you have a picture of the victim? Before he was killed?"

Annie pulled her phone out, tapping a few times to bring up a driver's license photo that she expanded to fill the screen and hide all other details on the license. I looked at the man staring uncomfortably back at me and felt the blood drain from my face.

"Do you know him?" she asked, reaching out as if to support me.

"He's a waiter, at a little Italian restaurant called Luigi's. I just saw him last night."

16

O llie took down the name of the restaurant in his notebook, while Annie looked up the number on her phone. I wanted to call them right then, to ask about when the waiter had left the night before and if anyone saw another person with him or following him. But Ollie said the detectives would handle that. He didn't want me giving them a reason to refuse to work with me.

They left soon after, draining the cups of coffee and then walking through my front door. Annie stopped a few steps away, turning to look at me with her eyes hidden behind mirrored sunglasses. "Be careful, Dahlish. Whatever is going on out there, it seems to be getting awful close to you."

I watched her walk to the patrol car, thinking about how she hadn't questioned it when Ollie and I were talking about the victims as if they were killed by some unknown *thing* instead of another person. I'd been afraid that after Ollie got saddled with a rookie, we might have to stop collaborating, but now I wondered if the young woman might not have already started figuring out what was really going on in the world around her.

I locked the door behind me after the patrol car pulled away from the curb, hurrying to my car parked in the drive. My next-door neighbor, an older retired woman who loved gardening so much that she had cultivated my own front yard and turned it into a masterpiece, waved at me. She was bent over a bed of plants that I knew produced beautiful pink and white blossoms around late March.

The first thing I did was plug my phone into the charger. Then I pressed the speed dial button I had set up and backed out of my driveway onto the street. After only two rings, Karen answered. "Jack, thank God. I was starting to worry about you when you didn't call me back."

"Sorry, Karen. I was exhausted for some reason last night. Dropped off as soon as I got home and didn't wake up until late this morning."

"Did you see Barbara last night?" she asked, her voice hesitant. I wondered if she was hoping I'd say no.

"Yeah, I showed up expecting to meet you and found her instead. I probably should have just left, but I didn't want to be rude to your sister. We had a short dinner."

"What did she say, Jack? What did she *do*?" She sounded almost despairing as she asked the questions. Suddenly, I had a hunch.

"Karen, did you have to move around a lot as kids because your sister kept sleeping with your boyfriends?"

"Oh my God, did she seduce you?"

Whoops. "No! Well, maybe a little, but I think it was more like she was trying to make sure I was really serious about you. She even asked me what my intentions were toward you."

"What did you say to that?"

"I said I loved you, that I wanted to have you in my life for years to come, and that I would never hurt you."

"Oh, Jack." Karen sounded sad, and I couldn't figure out why. Did she not feel as strongly about me? "I wish you wouldn't have told her that."

"Why? Karen, what's going on? I thought we've been really great together."

"We have. We are." She sighed, and I felt a sinking feeling in my stomach. I just knew I'd screwed things up somehow. It seemed to happen every time I started to think I'd found something that would last forever. "Jack, I love you more than I can say, and I'm very happy to hear that you love me. It's just my sister. You don't know what she's like."

"Tell me, Karen. You can talk to me."

"I want to, Jack, I really do. But this is something even you wouldn't understand. I'll handle it, just... I need you to stay away for a little while. Until I get Barbara back on her feet and out of town."

My car drifted to the curb as I brought it to a stop. My heart felt like someone had dropped a ton of bricks on it and they were jumping up and down to make sure it was completely crushed. "Let me help. Whatever it is, I can help you through it."

"No, Jack. This has always been a family matter, and it needs to stay that way."

I breathed deeply, trying to calm my emotions. The last thing I needed to do was start blubbering into the phone. "I guess I can understand that. Don't shut me out, though. Meet me tomorrow night, Karen. You're my valentine, remember?"

I could hear the faint smile in her voice, and that made me feel a little better. "I remember. Okay, we can have dinner tomorrow night. You never said where you were taking me."

"The first place we shared a meal," I said. It wasn't a fancy restaurant, but it was still the one place I could drive by and smile thinking about Karen.

"Good choice," she whispered, sounding happier. "I'll meet you there, at eight. And thank you, Jack. For understanding."

She ended the connection, and I sat there for several minutes gripping the wheel, trying to figure out what had caused the reaction. If she was mad at me for having dinner with her sister, then surely she wouldn't agree to the date tomorrow night. And what was it about Barbara that made Karen so nervous and sad?

Finally, I managed to pull my thoughts together and get back onto the road. As much as I was feeling crushed, there was work to be done and lives still in danger. Hopefully, I'd get Karen to open up to me on our date and find out what was making her act so strange all of a sudden.

It was half past noon when I pulled up to the waiter's apartment complex, after stopping to grab a burger I could eat in the car. I was feeling famished after fifteen hours of sleep, and my stomach's grumbles had become harder to ignore every time I passed a restaurant or fast-food place and got a whiff of what they were cooking.

There was a patrol car still sitting in the apartment office parking lot. The cop standing outside the driver's door walked over to look through my passenger window as I drove up. He was an officer I'd seen at crime scenes before, though I could never remember his name. Faces were easy for me to remember, while names seemed to slip right through my memory like water through a colander.

"Dahlish, right? Sergeant Williams said you might be by. Go on in. It's building twelve, and the unit is on the east end of the building."

"Thanks," I said with a wave, pulling forward through the gate that opened when he held out a small remote and pressed a button. I guessed he had been posted there to let forensics techs and detectives through whenever they showed up.

Finding the building was the hardest part. The complex was lined with trees, and branches had spread out to cover most of the numbers on the buildings. I passed buildings marked with 2, 5, and 9 without seeing anything in between, and started to wonder what kind of strange system had been established for numbering them. I finally found building twelve when I saw a black SUV from the crime lab parked in a fire lane.

I found an empty parking spot with ease, with most of the residents out at work or living their lives that afternoon. Sliding out from behind the steering wheel, I looked around at the parked cars and wondered which of them might have belonged to Gerald Jones when he was the waiter giving me disapproving glances the evening before.

Two of the forensics techs were still hovering around one of the balconies, and I walked closer to look at what was left. Namely, an outdoor chair with a thin green and white striped cushion that was covered in a brownish stain. I almost gagged as I thought about that being remnants of what Ollie had called a "juicy" body. I couldn't pick up any kind of decomposition smell, though.

"If you start showing up to all my crime scenes, I'm going to think you're sweet on me."

I turned at the voice to see dark eyes looking at me over a blue mask that covered her nose and mouth. I could tell she was smiling by the humps where her cheeks were hidden. "Hey, Mariah. Seen anything yet that would definitely tie in with the others?"

She glanced over at her partner, an older man who was combing through the hedges that ran along the front of the building. "Oh, this poor guy was killed by the same thing. I don't have any doubts on that."

"What about the state of the body? Ollie said he wasn't as dried out as the last two."

"That's true, there was still a bit of blood and moisture left. It looks like whatever was draining him must have been interrupted. Probably because they were stupid enough to do it out here on the patio." She waved at the small space, an eight by four concrete slab between two walls that formed part of the apartment. There was a barred railing across it, to maintain the illusion of privacy for anyone relaxing outside on the patio.

"Do we know yet what time it might have happened?"

"Couldn't have been more than a few hours before he was found." Mariah raised a hand to pull the mask down, scratching her nose once it was exposed. "That's better. It gets so hot under these things. Anyway, it's hard to really pin down time of death since whatever drains the body messes with the normal indicators we use, like liver temps. It couldn't have been when the woman found him and called it in, because the bodily fluid covering the chair cushions was already dry along the edges."

I shuddered, grateful I didn't have the job of determining how much of the liquid was still gooey. "I kind of assumed that early morning worker was the one who scared off our attacker, but it doesn't sound like it."

"Probably someone else passing by that didn't even look over. People coming home from bars or clubs, maybe. We'll know for sure this afternoon. Cavanaugh called the mayor and got a rush put on the autopsy. They'll be starting it soon, and that should give us a lot more information."

It was my turn to look around and make sure we were alone. I even remembered to look up, to verify no one was standing on their balcony listening to us. Even so, I still lowered my voice. "Mariah, did you have a chance to check for another one of those thorns or barbs?"

She shook her head. "Not yet. I checked the tongue and couldn't see anything there on a quick inspection. I couldn't very well just pull his penis out and feel it up with all the cops around."

"No, I guess that might have seemed a little odd." We shared a smile, both thinking about the absurdity of it when the entire situation was more than a little weird. It was the third body, though, and by now the cops were getting accustomed to seeing them and probably didn't spare much thought for how someone could end up like that.

"I'll call you when I hear anything, Jack. Cross my heart." She reached up and performed the action. I almost took the opportunity to ask about the old folktales about stakes to the heart, but decided it wasn't the best time.

"Thanks, Mariah. I really appreciate what you're doing for me on these cases. I owe you big time."

"I think I owe you, too." She looked at me from the corners of her eyes. "Uriah was very happy last night. He said the matriarch of the new family had finally been in contact. She agreed to a meeting with him and Emily Van Owen in a few nights."

I hunched down in my coat. "Yeah, I sort of forgot to tell you with some other stuff that happened. I met the head of the new clutch yesterday afternoon. Kind of crashed her kids' soccer practice, actually. We had a little chat, and I'm satisfied they aren't the ones doing all of this." I waved a hand at the stained chair on the patio. "I also mentioned it would be in her best interests to communicate with the Harrisons and Van Owens."

Mariah reached up to squeeze my arm. "Thank you, Jack. I was starting to worry about what might happen if they kept ignoring Uriah's attempts at contact. I probably shouldn't be telling you this, but he was getting a little paranoid that they had been sent by some enemies of his up north."

My fingers itched, wanting to pull out my notebook and start scribbling this down. If there was the potential of trouble coming to my city, that was something I needed to put some time into investigating. "This family came from the south, actually. Central America."

She smiled, pulling her mask back up to cover her nose and mouth. "Thanks for not pumping me for more information on what's up north. You're not a bad guy, Dahlish." She walked away jauntily, humming as she rejoined her partner to continue combing the grounds for any clues to find the killer.

As soon as she was gone, I did pull out my notebook and write a few lines to remind myself later on to look into the potential northern threat. I'd like to put down my bad memory to age, but it had been something I'd dealt with since childhood. My mom used to say it's because I had the attention span of a butterfly. At least that had improved over the years.

Slipping the notebook and short pen back into my coat pocket, I glanced around once more to be sure I was alone. I remembered how vivid things had been when I opened my senses at the soccer field the day before, and I really didn't want to experience that again with Mariah too close to me. She and her partner were out of sight beyond the edge of the building.

I reached up and touched the talisman as I slipped into the supernatural world, trying to ease into it as slowly as possible. The world around me instantly faded to misty background, as the essence trails snapped into sharp focus. I could see the black streaks where Mariah had stood moments earlier, as well as increasingly fainter trails of it where she had combed the crime scene over the last couple of hours. The blackness was everywhere, along with the smell of dirt and death.

Unlike the first crime scene, it didn't obscure the other essence underneath. As soon as I picked up on the faint pink trails, they seemed to shift forward and become more substantial as the vampire essence faded along with the real world. The smell of peach blossoms overwhelmed everything else, and I felt drowsiness touching the edges of my mind. For some reason, this time I was able to resist it and keep my attention focused.

The pink trailing essence was strongest on this side of the patio railing. As I looked over, the patio itself became clearer and less insubstantial. The outdoor chair seemed to almost be spotlighted, as I noticed the way the pink essence appeared to lean forward toward it. I could imagine sitting there, enjoying the fresh cold air after a long night at work, when someone approached the railing. Maybe they asked a question, or maybe they just wanted to talk, but I would lean forward to hear their whispered voice more clearly as they leaned in toward me. Until our faces almost met.

I wasn't sure where that image had come from, but I was suddenly certain it was what had happened. Jerry had been approached by someone he either recognized or deemed harmless. I couldn't imagine that would apply to many people who approached you in the early hours at your home. That's usually when people are most guarded and careful.

Turning my head, I could see the pink trail heading for the parking lot. I followed it, stunned by how strong and vibrant it was against the background of the washed-out human world. I even felt as if I could confidently say that it had been left eight to ten hours earlier. There was something about the raggedness along the edges that made that clear in my mind even as I wondered how I could know it.

I passed my car, a low pulsing beacon from within the supernatural world, and had to stop and gape in open-mouthed wonder. It was almost like the sun had been captured within, and yellow rays of light were shooting from the windows. They faded within a foot or so, but it made my vehicle instantly visible.

I shook off that fascination, dragging my attention back onto the pink trail I was following. It kept going, through the parking lot and past two more buildings, before it stopped on the white strip separating two parking spaces. The Nox that created it had climbed out of and back into a car there, but I couldn't tell which side of a car they might have entered. No way to know if they'd been driving or just riding along as someone else drove.

With no more than a thought, I departed the supernatural world and reality snapped back into focus. That was when I felt my first wave of nausea and realized I hadn't felt it the entire time I was detecting the Nox essences. I also hadn't felt the lulling effects of the essence that had been so debilitating at the previous crime scenes. There were a lot of implications there, things that would require a lot of thought that I didn't have time for in that moment.

As I walked back to my car, I turned my thoughts back to the victim. Whoever had drained him had come here specifically for him. That pink trail had not wavered as it arrowed straight for his apartment. In fact, as I stopped beside the patio again, I noticed that anyone would have to pass by on the way to where Jerry's door was in the breezeway around the corner of the building. So maybe the killer had been heading there, happened to see the waiter sitting on his patio, and took advantage in the moment. It would explain why they attacked out in the open.

That was a lot of new information that I didn't have an hour earlier, but none of it got me any closer to finding my killer. I'd have to be patient and wait to hear from Mariah or Ollie with the results of the autopsy. If they could find that same barb or thorn, that would cinch it as the way the killer was draining the bodies. I just had to figure out what kind of Nox would leave behind such a trace.

17

A s I sat in my office chair, watching the stream of tourists below walking between La Villita and the Riverwalk, I couldn't stop thinking about Gerald Jones. Jerry the waiter. A man I had seen and spoken with several times on trips to Luigi's. How did he fit in with the other two victims? What made the killer target him? I had a suspicion it was related to me somehow, but I couldn't figure it out.

I went back to the first victim. His name was Walter Johnson, a patriotic kid who enlisted in the army right out of high school and got swept up in the Vietnam War. He survived it, coming away with the same painful memories and post-traumatic stress of most other veterans of the conflict, but had remained in the military. He served for twenty-five years, reaching the rank of Master Sergeant before he retired and settled down in the city of his last posting. Married in his late twenties, widowed before he was fifty. No siblings or children, and his parents had been deceased for years.

According to all of his neighbors, he lived a quiet life. Walter volunteered at his church and with the Food Bank, took on the occasional job doing event security to supplement his retirement income, and was friendly with everyone on his street. His closest neighbors had mentioned seeing women at the house a few times over the last couple of years, but rarely more than once. They assumed it was dating attempts that didn't pan out.

Ollie said the police suspected they'd been escorts. Not that they could find any trace of it in the man's financials.

The second victim, Martin Ogelvy, also lived alone. A life-long bachelor, the closest he'd ever come to settling down had been an engagement in his thirties. According to his sister, the only sibling and the person who sent him postcards from her vacations that ended up on his fridge, the engagement had fallen through when the woman was discovered to be sleeping with several other men. That had soured Martin on the dating experience.

He'd moved into the Castle Hills neighborhood only two years ago, keeping to himself most of the time. Few of the other people on the street knew much about him, except as a face they recognized when they saw him. He seemed to spend a lot of his time at work, an insurance company where he evaluated claims and decided whether to pay out or not. That alone would have been enough to generate more than a few enemies in his life, but according to the company, they kept the identity of the decision makers anonymous.

The people who lived on either side of his house said they had never seen any friends or female visitors. Which made it all the stranger that he would have ordered food for two people the night he died. There had to be something to that coincidence, both of the first victims ordering food delivery the night they died. And both of them ordering enough food for more than one person. Ollie said the detectives on the case were already trying to find out if the men had been members of the same dating site, and maybe met their killer that way. It was definitely the time of year for something like that, with no one wanting to be alone on Valentine's Day.

Gerald Jones was the deviation on the pattern. For one, he lived in an apartment complex where it was much harder to get privacy. Even when you were inside, the people above or to the sides could hear any loud voices or noises. His neighbors, though, said they loved having Jerry near them. He was always considerate about noise when he'd come home late from work, and he was usually up living his life while they were away from home at their jobs.

There was also no way he'd have been on any of the same dating sites as the previous victims. Jerry had come out after his divorce. He was dating a man who worked as a line cook at the same restaurant where he was a waiter. In fact, the boyfriend said they'd spent half an hour together after they left work the previous evening. It had been almost two in the morning before Jerry headed home alone.

I couldn't stop thinking that there had to be some connection between him and me. I looked at my phone and saw that it was late enough that Luigi's would be opening soon for the dinner crowd; they closed between two and four every day. The cops had already been by to question the coworkers that morning, so I felt confident I could get in and ask some questions of my own without stepping on any toes.

As I drove to the restaurant, my mind started to wander into areas I was trying to avoid. Namely, Karen and the call we'd had that morning. I still couldn't figure out why she suddenly decided we needed to take a break. As much as I didn't want it to, it made me hate her sister just a little. Everything was going great until Barbara showed up. That's when Karen started to dwell on her past. And that had been the reason she wanted me to keep my distance for a while. What had her sister done when they were younger that made her so afraid that her return was going to ruin things? I couldn't help but think my guess had been right, that Barbara had a habit of sleeping with her sister's boyfriends. Maybe it was sibling jealousy.

Pulling into Luigi's parking lot, I shoved those worries aside and forced myself to focus on the case. If I could find this killer, then I could spend more time trying to get Karen to open up and tell me what was going on. I took deep breaths as I walked through the lot, clearing my head.

When I pushed through the restaurant's door, I was greeted almost instantly by the man standing behind the short counter just inside. He was average sized, a decade older than me, and impeccably dressed in a nice suit. Antonio, the owner of the restaurant and the man I'd been hoping to speak with. Yeah, I was kind of surprised he wasn't named Luigi, too.

"Ah, Mr. Dahlish. Will Ms. Kilgraff be joining you this afternoon?"

"I'm on my own today, Antonio. I was actually hoping I could speak with you and some of the staff. About Jerry."

His smile dropped away, and I noticed the dark circles under his eyes for the first time. "Oh, it is such a terrible thing, Mr. Dahlish. Why would anyone want to hurt such a nice man?"

"That's what I'm hoping to find out. I'm working on the investigation with the police," I told him, fibbing just a little.

His eyes brightened instantly. "That is wonderful news. I'm sure you'll find this monster in no time." He leaned in, lowering his voice as he looked around the almost empty restaurant. "Between you and me, the detectives that were in this morning did not inspire much confidence. They seemed more concerned with Jerry's sexual persuasion than anything else."

I sniffed, shaking my head. "That's why I'm here. I'll let them work angles like that, while I focus on areas that make more sense. For instance, do you know if Jerry had any regulars that he might have talked to often? People that might have known how to find where he lived?"

Antonio tapped his chin for a second, then held up a hand and waved for a waitress to come over and take his place. Once she was ensconced behind the counter to greet customers, he motioned for me to follow to a table in the rear corner of the dining area. He held out a chair for me, and then asked if I'd like something to drink while we spoke. I almost laughed at how he slipped into the waiter personality so easily.

He brought a pitcher of water and a couple of glasses over, then sat across from me. "Jerry did have quite a few regulars, people who would ask to be seated in his section if he was working. He was very good at talking with the customers, making them feel welcome and relaxed as they ordered or after their meals. But I've never heard him give personal details about himself, Mr. Dahlish. As much as I hate to say it, we in the restaurant business learn early on to not give out too much information."

That made sense. After all, I didn't have to think too hard to come up with half a dozen examples of waiters and waitresses that were targeted by stalkers who thought their friendliness at work was an invitation for something more. "Were any of those regulars in here last night?"

Antonio chuckled, and nodded toward the table I had been seated at twenty-four hours earlier. "Just you, Mr. Dahlish. I must say that you were the talk of the kitchen, meeting that attractive young woman. We were all convinced that you were stepping out on Ms. Kilgraff, until she told Jerry after you left that she was her sister."

Great, my personal life was the source of gossip. I'd never be able to not think about that when I stopped in to eat. Not that it would prevent me from doing so. The mushroom ravioli was that good. "Barbara stayed and talked to Jerry after I left?"

"Oh yes, she was here for another hour, maybe a bit longer. She drew the interest of quite a few gentlemen, but she didn't seem to be concerned with them." His eyes grew hooded, and he looked away as if trying to decide something.

"What is it, Antonio?"

"Well... Mr. Dahlish, she was mostly asking questions about you. She asked Jerry how often you came here, and if you were ever with someone other than Ms. Kilgraff. Then she asked Jerry how the two of you appeared when you were together. If you were in love or just friendly."

That was pretty strange. I wasn't sure what to make of it, but I didn't like the direction my instincts were pushing me. "Did she ever ask Jerry about himself? Maybe who he was dating or where he lived?"

"Not that I know of." Antonio shook his head regretfully. "I really only know what Jerry and Margaret, the other server on duty last night, said when they were in the kitchen while I was."

"Could I get a phone number for Margaret? I'd like to see if she heard anything more."

Antonio raised his head, and I turned to see the waitress that had taken his place behind the counter. I really needed to start checking name tags. "I'll have her come over, but don't keep her too long, Mr. Dahlish. The next customers will be seated in her section."

I promised not to take up too much of her time, and he left me to join her at the counter. He spoke to her quietly, motioning toward me, and she began walking toward me with a quizzical expression. I stood to greet her and waved her into the seat across from mine.

"Thanks for talking with me, Margaret. Antonio said you overheard some of the conversation between Jerry and the young woman last night?"

"You mean the woman you had dinner with, sir? Yes, I heard bits of it. I have the row of booths against this wall." She gestured toward the wall not far away, the row of booths that led from the entrance to the rear of the dining room. It was very close to the table where I'd been seated the day before.

"Did you happen to hear if she asked Jerry anything about himself? Could he have told her where he lived?"

She was taken aback. "We never do that, sir. One of the big rules of waiting tables is to keep yourself to yourself. Most people don't care to hear about our lives, and the ones who do are the people you never want to know anything about you."

"What were they talking about when you happened to overhear?"

Margaret thought about it for several seconds, which I appreciated. Most people just blurted out whatever was at the forefront of their mind, and then had to backtrack when I pressed them for events they had witnessed themselves and hadn't heard about from other people. "A few times, I heard the woman talking about Karen Kilgraff. That reporter you dine with now and then. She seemed to know her, but I didn't know how until Jerry told me in the kitchen that she was Ms. Kilgraff's sister.

"Another time, I heard the woman ask him about you. I was listing the specials for booth six, but I do that so often I barely even think about it anymore. So, I was able to pay attention when I heard her ask if you were ever here with someone else. Jerry doesn't... didn't like talking about other customers, but he did assure her that you were never here with anyone but Ms. Kilgraff."

"How did she seem to react to that? Was she happy to hear it, or upset?"

"I think she was satisfied to hear it. Not really happy, but as if she'd been hoping he would tell her that."

"Did you happen to hear her say anything when Jerry wasn't at the table? Or notice anything about her?"

Margaret hesitated, biting her lower lip in the way I'd seen many women do when they were thinking. "I glanced over once, while I was delivering drinks to booth four. The woman seemed to be watching Jerry, and she had this look in her eyes that struck me as odd. It's how people look when they're picking out items on the menu and find the one thing they've been craving. Does that make sense?"

Too much sense. "Yes, Margaret. Thank you for telling me."
I smiled reassuringly, knowing she was feeling uncomfortable to
be talking about another customer. I had a feeling she would
have refused to say anything at all if her boss hadn't let her know
I could be trusted. "One last thing. Jerry stayed late last night
with his boyfriend, right? Was that normal?"

She giggled, hiding her laugh behind a hand. "Very normal.
Jerry and Vic thought it was exciting to make out in the kitchen
after everyone left. I came back once after I forgot my phone
and surprised them. They're such a cute couple." Her face fell
as she realized Jerry wouldn't be doing anything like that again.

I gave her a few seconds, and then gently asked if Vic was
in. I was kind of surprised when she said he was, and she offered
to ask him if he would speak with me. For a moment, I had to
wonder what kind of boyfriend would show up for work the day
after the man he loved was killed, but then I realized that focusing on work had pushed my own worries about Karen aside. Vic
could be the kind of guy that preferred having something else to
focus on for a little while.

I wasn't sure what I expected a line cook to look like, but
Vic was not it. He was a small guy, thin and quiet. The kind of
person that naturally fades into the background, even when out
with friends or family. I'd seen chefs on TV, and they always
seemed loud and obnoxious.

"Thanks for taking a few minutes to speak with me. I'm
truly sorry for your loss."

"Thank you, Mr. Dahlish. Margaret said you're helping the
police find out who killed... who did that to Jerry?"

"Yes. I've been thinking that it must have been someone he met here at the restaurant. Did he ever talk to you about any customers that seemed creepy, or freaked him out in any way?"

Vic shook his head, his eyes flitting up to meet mine for a nanosecond before falling back to the tablecloth. "No, sir. There are a few people he enjoys talking to when they come in. But no one that really worries him." He grimaced. "*Worried* him."

For a moment, I felt tempted to walk over and give the kid a hug. I knew how hard it was to think about someone and constantly realize you were never going to see them again or listen to their voice. I'd gone through the same thing with my sister ten years ago. "When he left last night, did he say anything strange? Or act like he might be expecting someone to visit his home?"

He looked indignant for a second, but it faded quickly. "Jerry would never cheat on me, Mr. Dahlish. Never."

"I didn't mean to imply that, Vic. Really. It's just that... did the cops tell you anything about how Jerry died?"

His eyes were growing wet, and I saw the first tear slide down his cheek as he shook his head. "They said someone killed him at his home, but they wouldn't tell me how or why."

"The why part we're still working on. And trust me, you don't want to know the how. I'll just say that I don't think he felt much of it. But he was out on his patio, Vic. It looked like he had gone to sit out there after work, and someone approached him."

Vic smiled briefly before it faded from his lips. "Jerry loved to sit on the patio late at night. He swore he could see the stars from his chair, even though I never saw more than a few through the trees and light pollution. It was his place to sit and unwind after work, de-stress before he went to bed."

"Sounds nice," I said, knowing they had probably shared many nights there together.

"It was." He looked up at me again, maintaining eye contact for several seconds this time. "I was supposed to be there, Mr. Dahlish. We'd planned to go back to Jerry's place after work last night, but then I had something come up and had to spend this morning with my mother. I told him we'd do it tonight instead, and we spent half an hour together here before going our separate ways." His hands clenched on the tablecloth, knuckles white. "Why didn't I go home with him? I could have stopped whatever happened!"

I reached across to place a hand over his. "Maybe, Vic. You also could have been killed alongside him, leaving your family feeling as devastated as you do right now. It might have changed nothing at all."

"But I'll never know, and I'll never be able to forget that I could have saved his life." His body started to shake with sobs, and I looked around helplessly. Antonio was rushing over, and he grabbed Vic's shoulders to guide him out of the chair and toward the kitchen.

Several steps away, the cook stopped and turned to look at me with beseeching eyes. "Find whatever monster took Jerry away from me, Mr. Dahlish. Find them, and maybe I can live with myself for not being there when he needed me most."

I nodded, lips tight as I fought against my own emotion. As much as I'd wanted to find the killer before, I wanted it even more now. For Vic and Jerry, and what could have been. I flipped my notebook closed and slid it back into my pocket, standing and pushing my chair in against the table before I left.

A voice caught me before I pulled the door open, making me turn. Margaret was standing behind me, her hands twisting together. "Mr. Dahlish, there's one thing I remembered. I don't know how it could help you at all, but I have to say it."

"Go ahead," I told her, stepping aside so we weren't interrupted by any arriving customers. "What is it, Margaret?"

"That woman, the one you had dinner with? She got a call when Jerry was in the kitchen. I only heard bits of what she said, but I know she told the person on the phone that she would be back late, not to wait up. It wasn't so much what she said as how she said it. You know, kind of gloating like she had won one over on the other person."

I thanked her for telling me, smiling to let her know that it was appreciated. Inside, my stomach was roiling. I'd walked into the restaurant trying to find a connection, and left wishing I weren't so sure that I now knew what it was.

18

B ack inside my car, with the engine on and the heaters blowing, I tried calling Karen. The phone rang four times and then went to her voicemail. This wasn't the kind of thing I wanted to leave as a message, so I hung up and tried calling again. When I got voicemail a second time, I tossed the phone down with frustration.

I knew I had to speak with Karen. She was the only one who could tell me if what I now suspected about Barbara were true. At the same time, I couldn't believe that her sister could be a Nox. That would make Karen one, as well, and surely I would have detected such a thing in all our time together. I hadn't blinded myself entirely, had I?

It was almost five thirty. I wondered if Karen might have stepped in to anchor the weekend news. She was a workaholic and would often offer to take a day if someone else needed time off, so it wasn't unreasonable. I pulled up the KRSA website, tapping the link for *Watch Live*. Not long after first meeting Karen, I had signed up with the site so I could watch her broadcasts any time I was sitting in the car on stakeouts or working late in my office.

The video buffered for half a minute as I goaded it under my breath. "Come on, you piece of junk. Freaking play already." Finally, I was able to watch the last few minutes of the news. The woman sitting at the desk, laughing and joking with the male anchor and sportscaster, was not Karen. That meant she was probably at home, but I didn't know where that was. For the first time, I realized that she had smoothly diverted my attention any time I mentioned picking her up before a date or bringing a meal over. Now I had to wonder if she had something to hide from me, and I hated that feeling.

I called her number again, hoping she might have just been busy before and would answer this time. It rang four times and went to voicemail again. Muttering under my breath, I started tapping through my home screen to find the icon for one of the information services I used most. It made me feel dirty even thinking about it, but I would have to run a search on Karen and see if I could turn up a home address. This was too important.

The screen flashed as I got an incoming call. My heart soared, until I saw it was an unknown caller and not Karen calling me back. I almost stabbed the ignore button, but something inside me guided my finger to slide the green button across the screen.

"What?!" I yelled into the phone, angry at whoever was interrupting me.

"We found him," came the lilting reply. "Your friend's spelunking source called him thirty minutes ago. She came across a large cavern deep down a rarely explored branch of the cave system. There was a light, and she saw movement before she pulled back."

"Padraig, I don't have time for this right now. I have three dead people, and I think I just figured out who's been doing it."

"I have hundreds of dead people, Dahlish. And I *know* who did it and where he is. You promised to help, and I expect you to honor that."

I slammed my hand against the steering wheel a few times. Why did everything always seem to happen at once? "Fine, I'll do as I promised. But you have to help me when we're done. Where should I meet you?"

"We're already on the way," he said, and I realized I could hear muted traffic sounds in the background. "Nyk said he just sent you a text with the location."

I pulled the phone away from my ear, pressing the button to switch programs. Nyk's message was waiting, with a link that opened my map program to show the destination. It was a small parking lot far from any heavily traveled locations.

"Okay, I'm on the way."

With the phone guiding me, I pulled out of the restaurant's parking lot and headed for the interstate. Once there, I tried calling Karen again. If I could just get her to answer, then maybe she could tell me how wrong my idea was, and we could always laugh about the time Jack was a total moron for an hour.

I got her voicemail again, and this time I told her that it was important, and I needed her to call me back. Too late, I remembered that I would soon be underground and wouldn't have reception. I almost called back to leave another message, but I thought that would just make it sound desperate instead of urgent.

It took almost forty minutes to reach the location Nyk had directed me to. We were deep in the hill country here, and the few houses I had passed on this road had several acres separating them. This was where people lived when they didn't want to know their neighbors, or to discourage people dropping in unexpectedly.

As I pulled into the small parking lot, I saw the bounty hunter's monster truck sitting under the only tree that shaded the lot. It was a double cab truck, the kind with two wheels on either side of the rear axle, and it was jacked a good two feet off the ground. Toddlers could have played underneath it without fear of hitting their heads.

Padraig was leaning against the rear bumper and raised a hand in greeting as I pulled up beside him. "The big fella is out there," he said, waving toward the trees and brush in front of the parked vehicles. "Getting the lowdown from his friend, who's too good for the likes of us, apparently."

"Sources like to keep their anonymity until they feel they can trust someone new," I said. I had more than a few people like that who would feed me information off and on. They usually wanted to meet in a crowded public place, where they'd pretend they didn't know me at all as they dropped a note for me to pick up. But some of them liked to meet in secluded areas, where they could talk without worrying that someone they knew might happen by and see us together.

Nyk appeared a few minutes later, moving lightly for someone so large. His steps were almost delicate, as if he were trying to leave no trace of his passing. It gave me a chill to think of someone like that on my trail, and I almost sympathized with the people he was hired to track down.

"Okay," he said as he stepped onto the paved lot. "The entrance we're using is about half a mile southwest of here. Sonia is willing to guide us, but you have to listen to everything she says." He looked at Padraig, waiting for the Irishman to nod in reluctant agreement. Nyk then reached out to pull his tailgate down, exposing the covered bed of his truck. He pulled out a large container, setting it on the ground and taking the lid off to reveal ropes and harnesses. There was also headgear that looked like faceless football helmets with mounted lights.

Sonia appeared then, a small woman who looked to have Native American heritage. I later learned she was half Kiowa, on her father's side. She was no more than a few inches over five feet, with slender limbs that looked ideal for squeezing through tight spaces.

She helped us all put on the safety gear, spending half an hour getting us into thick suits that were waterproof and would protect our arms and legs as we rubbed against rough stone. Harnesses went over the suits, with a series of carabiners we would use to connect ourselves together with the ropes. "The last thing I need is to have to explain to my bosses how I lost some wannabe caver. You *will* stay attached to a rope at all times. Give it three strong tugs if you get into trouble or feel you need assistance."

We also carried backup batteries for our headlamps, and a small flashlight we could use in emergencies. A hydration pack was strapped onto our backs under the suits, with a thin tube in the collar we could use to drink when necessary. "Trust me on this, the last thing you want is to get dehydrated down there. You may feel fine, but before you know it, you'll be disoriented and lose all sense of direction. That's not something you want happening deep in a cave."

Nyk grinned over at me, knowing I was already bad at directions. Without the sun as reference, I honestly couldn't have told anyone which way was west from where we were standing in that parking lot. I usually had to stop and think about where the roads were in the city when I needed to know which direction to face.

"I've laid down some guide ropes," Sonia continued. "We'll have those to follow for most of the trip, but I couldn't risk making noise too close to where your man is. Nyk told me he's dangerous, and that I shouldn't be seen."

"Got that right, sister," Padraig said under his breath.

She took a look at us, and I could see from her eyes that she'd been working long hours on too little sleep. If not for the urgency to find the jotunn before he could kill more people, I would have suggested we wait until morning, so she didn't fall asleep guiding us through dark caves deep underground. Maybe a little of that was my own fear of being trapped with thousands of tons of rock hanging over my head, and no idea how to get out. Nyk and Padraig didn't seem to share that hesitation, and I could see both almost straining to be off.

"Take ten minutes and make sure you have everything," Sonia said, holding up a finger when Padraig opened his mouth to protest another delay. "You don't want to hear me list all the times that ten minutes have saved lives down there. And drink up before we go in." She pulled some bottled waters from the backpack at her feet, passing them around.

While the others talked about what might be most needed in the caves, I hurried back to my car where I'd left my phone on the hood as I was changing. I'd hoped to see a missed call from Karen, or even a text, but there was nothing. I called again, getting her voice mail for the fifth time. I was starting to feel really concerned now, with no response from her. Even if she were upset with me for some reason, I thought she would have checked in to see what was worrying me. Karen knew me well enough to know I wouldn't freak out over trivialities.

I typed in a quick message that shouldn't raise alarm bells if Barbara happened to see it. *Third victim today. Worried about case, please call me.* Hopefully, Karen would realize I had something related to those deaths to talk about. If nothing else, the reporter in her should be very curious to hear what I had to say.

My phone slid neatly into a small pocket on the thigh of the suit I was wearing. As I walked over to rejoin the others, I kept running a hand over the rough fabric. It felt almost like a mix between corduroy pants and a neoprene wetsuit. It was also nice and warm, keeping me from shivering in the growing cold of night without my jacket, which I had tucked neatly into my trunk to keep it safe. Don't laugh, it was the most expensive piece of clothing I'd ever owned, and I was a little overprotective.

"Last chance to back out," Sonia said, picking up her backpack and slinging the straps over her shoulders.

"We're ready," Padraig assured her. "I've been waiting on this for months." I couldn't tell if his lips were pulled back in a snarl or expectant grin, but either way it sent a shiver down my spine.

Sonia led us through brush and trees, following a faint trail by the light of our headlamps. I was silently praying we didn't step on a rattlesnake in the dark, even though I knew they had to be holed up somewhere to keep warm. That's about the time I started wondering if the place they holed up was in the caves and crevices we were about to descend into. I'd always hated snakes, and almost getting killed by a lamia in an earlier case hadn't improved my feelings about them.

A quarter of an hour later, we were standing around a crack in the ground. Sonia dropped her backpack through the hole, and then started to wiggle into it herself. I kept looking around, hoping to find a large entrance in the side of a hill like you always see in movies. Padraig dropped through second, easily slipping through the crevice. "It's wider once you get inside," he called out.

I looked up at Nyk, the man least likely to fit through most of the tight spaces we'd been warned about. He was eyeing the small crack in the ground, but finally shrugged and crouched down to slide first one leg and then the other into it. As I watched him slowly disappear, I was reminded of videos I'd watched of snakes eating animals twice as large as they were.

Once his head disappeared into the blackness, I looked up at the starry sky and sighed deeply. "Jack versus his sudden claustrophobia. A case for the ages." Before I could think about it any further, I sat down and stuck a foot through the crack.

19

Padraig was right. Once inside the small cave mouth, it opened up into a comfortable space. It was tight with all four of us filling the space, but looking up at the crack I'd come through helped whenever I started to feel a tightness in my chest.

"Our path is this way," Sonia said, pointing her headlamp toward an opening in the wall that had been invisible in the near darkness. I could see the first spike planted in the wall, holding a blue and yellow rope that was knotted on the end so it wouldn't slide through the clip. There were a couple of other knots below that at intervals of a foot apart, and I wondered if that was in case the first worked loose. How hard would we be tugging on the rope as we worked our way deeper into the caves?

Sonia led the way, with Padraig close behind in his eagerness to catch up to the jotunn. I wasn't sure why he was in such a hurry, if he hadn't been able to stop Surtr with a group of mercenaries. Nyk brought a lot of power to our small party, but it couldn't match up with a bunch of people carrying automatic weapons. I wasn't sure I added much, either.

I stayed behind Nyk, knowing that the big man would probably need a few helpful shoves when we got to tight spaces. A part of me might have even been hoping that he'd get stuck somewhere and I'd have to regretfully be left out of the confrontation with a creature that had killed hundreds of people over the last seven months. I knew that was my old self talking, though, and it was easy to shove that voice into the background.

The tunnel we were following branched off a couple of times during the first half hour, but Sonia confidently followed the rope she had laid down earlier in the day. I could see small divots in the rock walls of other tunnels where she must have strung the rope until she verified there was nothing of interest at the end of it.

I was already grateful for the suits Sonia had made Nyk buy for us. My arms and legs kept scraping against rough protrusions from the rock wall, and I knew I'd be bleeding in several places if not for the protective fabric. There would still be bruises, but I'd happily take the lesser of two evils at this point. Or so I was thinking as I missed seeing Nyk duck in front of me and then slammed into a short stalactite. Stars flashed across my vision, and I reached up to slap a hand over my forehead. I was going to have a headache, but at least it didn't break skin thanks to our slow pace.

"You okay, Jack?"

"Yeah, just learning to pay more attention."

Nyk laughed, a low rumble deep in his chest, as he turned back to the tunnel and continued along the path. I couldn't stop admiring the way the bounty hunter could sinuously move through the tunnel, seemingly avoiding every bump and protrusion that I slammed my body into. When this was over, I'd have to ask him to take me along to yoga or whatever gave him such graceful movement.

It took more than an hour to reach the first stopping point, a small area where the tunnel widened enough for all of us to sit and drink from our water pouches. Every step we took deeper into the caves seemed to be warmer than the last. I had naturally assumed the caves would be just as cold as the air outside, but when I asked Sonia she just laughed.

"Not at all, most caves tend to be the same as the average ambient temperature of the region. The rock is such a good insulator that it doesn't vary by much no matter the season. So, you'd be feeling cooler in summer, but warmer now that it's winter. These caves tend to stick somewhere around seventy degrees or a bit higher. The humidity levels down here are higher than aboveground, as well."

That sounded like a comfortable temperature, the kind of weather that made me love spring and fall so much. But I didn't walk around in a heavy suit that was already making me sweat. I was starting to understand why she'd harped on hydration so much before we entered the caves.

We rested for five minutes before Padraig was on his feet and urging us forward again. The Irishman was getting impatient, when I'd have expected him to be more wary and measured as he prepared to face a foe that had defeated him at least once already and left him in a hospital for more than a week. Sonia was reluctant to move so soon but was eventually goaded to lead us deeper into the caves.

At the next branching, we found ourselves in a tunnel that was little more than a jagged crack in the rock. It was a tight fit, and Nyk especially had to struggle to push his body through a few spots. The floor was on a definite downward slope, as well, making it even harder to move forward when one of us got stuck. I had to shove Nyk a few times to get him through difficult squeezes, and once he had to return the favor by pulling my arm until I slipped through a point where I'd felt as if my chest was pinned between giant boulders.

When the tunnel began to widen again, I thought we might have made it past the worst part. And then I hated myself for tempting fate, as the ceiling started to slope down until we were crawling on our hands and knees. Not too bad for the first twenty or thirty feet, but then my knees started to scream at me that they weren't made for this kind of abuse. I was grateful for the small amount of padding in the suits that at least provided minimal cushioning.

"It's going to get a little tight pretty soon," Sonia called back.

"Pretty soon?" I asked quietly, my voice echoing until everyone heard my question.

"Trust me," she said, "what you're experiencing right now is a spelunker's dream. We've made it a touch more than a mile in the last hour, which is like driving eighty on a freeway. It's going to get much more difficult."

"How far is it to the cave our fugitive is in?" Padraig asked.

"Another mile to go."

I groaned but kept moving forward as the rock overhead continued pushing down further and further. Soon, I was on my stomach, pulling myself forward and using only the tips of my toes to push. Thankfully, the crevice we were crawling through was wide and Nyk didn't have too much difficulty. A few times I had to provide leverage for his large boots so he could push through a tight spot.

For a long time, the air was filled with grunts and exclamations when one of us jammed against a bit of rock sticking down from above. More than once, my suit got snagged on a stalactite and I had to almost yank it loose because I was too exhausted to shimmy backwards and then have to struggle through those couple of feet again. Getting through the tight tunnel was worse than any workout I'd suffered in a gym, and my muscles were starting to burn in protest.

On top of that, there were too many times that I had to stop, close my eyes, and just breathe. Times when my chest was feeling tight and the panic was trying to claw its way out of my body in a scream of terror. Walking through the wide-open caves of the tourist portion of Natural Bridge was vastly different from feeling thousands of tons of rock touching every part of your body and knowing it would take a microsecond for something to shift and trap you there forever.

It seemed to be hours later when the tunnel began to rise above our heads again. Even longer before I could get off my stomach, and then finally sit up against the wall with my head tilted down because the ceiling was still too low. We probably should have continued forward to a better resting place, but most of us were completely exhausted after the effort and needed a break. Sonia didn't protest too much, either, as she sipped her water.

"You do this kind of thing every day?" Padraig asked, a new respect in his voice.

"I wish!" Sonia said with a snort. "We get to explore and check for cave-ins three or four times a year. Usually, it takes a week to ten days for our group to make it through the previously explored cave system, and then we might spend another day or two trying to map out a new portion."

"I don't know how you do it," the Irishman said. "I'm already dreading the thought of having to go back through there on our way out."

That was something I hadn't considered yet, and I turned to look back along the tunnel where the narrow crevice was hidden in darkness. I shuddered, thinking of having to do it all over again.

"That wasn't even the worst part," Sonia said, amusement in her voice.

We felt really cheered by that news, excited to keep going and find new adventures. I would have turned back then, if not for the promise to my fellow talisman bearer. Instead, I pulled together all my willpower and followed the others as we continued deeper into the rock.

"We're only a couple hundred feet from where the rope guide ends," Sonia told us as we kept crawling. "But this is going to be the real test of how much you want this fugitive of yours." She came to a stop, and I leaned over to look beyond Nyk's bulk to see a solid rock wall. Our guide was pointing up.

"You have got to be kidding me," Padraig said, his eyes wide as he looked at the slanted opening near the ceiling that led up.

"Just be glad it's not straight up," she said, before she shimmied her body up and into the hole. "There are plenty of places to use as hand- and foot-holds, but go slow and make sure of your grip before pulling up to the next one."

Her voice became more of an echo as her feet disappeared, and Padraig looked back at me with a shrug before following after her. Once he was gone, Nyk and I turned our lights on the shaft. "Think you can make it?" I asked him.

"I have to try," he said, grabbing some gravelly soil to rub between his large hands. "I'm not letting you face a jotunn without me, Jack." He grinned, then stood up and started to disappear into the hole.

Left alone, I looked back along the way we had come. I was surprised I didn't even feel more than a twinge of desire to escape that way and race back to San Antonio and Karen. Worry about her and what Barbara might do was still running through my head, but I also knew Surtr was the larger threat at the moment. I hated it, but I had to place the greater good over the woman I loved.

The shaft proved easier to climb than I'd feared. Sonia had been right about the handholds, ridges in the rock that I guessed had been formed by water flowing down the shaft over thousands of years. I realized we were lucky it had been a dry winter, or we might have been making this trip through a trickling stream of cold water. Surely that was why the suits we wore were waterproof as well as protective for our bodies.

My fingers were screaming at me by the time I made it to the top of the shaft, carrying most of my weight every time I moved a foot to try and find a new toehold. If the shaft hadn't been at a forty-degree angle, I really didn't think I could have made it all the way up. As it was, I had to roll over on my back and just lie there for a few moments once I was back on mostly flat ground.

"Please tell me that was the worst part," I huffed.

"Absolutely," Sonia said with a smile. "There are still some tight squeezes, but that's the only spot you have to do any climbing. Believe me, it's a lot easier going down on the way out."

"Small victories," I said, holding up a hand in weak triumph.

Once we were moving again, it didn't take long to find the place where the rope guide ended. It was knotted again, to keep it connected to the spike in the rock wall. Looking at that, I had a thought. "Wouldn't Surtr have heard the noise when you pounded all these spikes into the wall?" I reached out to touch the cool metal, where it was flattened from years of hammer blows.

"Sound echoes a lot in here," Sonia said. "It seems really loud when you're close, but if you were a hundred feet down the tunnel, you'd barely hear it. Also, there's a small waterfall in the cave your fugitive is using, and that noise covers a lot."

That was good news, at least. Less chance of us barging in on a jotunn prepared after listening to our advance for half an hour or more. Padraig nodded, and I could see that he'd been concerned about the same thing. The fact that he hadn't voiced it made me wonder if he would have charged in regardless.

The tunnel we were in after climbing the shaft was large enough that we could stand up, though Nyk and I had to duck slightly to keep our heads from banging against the rock ceiling. That allowed us to move faster than we had during the long stretch of crawling and climbing. I pulled my phone out of the compartment in my thigh, grateful to see it hadn't taken a beating so far. It wasn't a huge surprise to see that I had no bars, and no missed call or text message notifications.

A noise I'd been hearing soon revealed itself to be a trickling stream of water, running along the edge of the tunnel floor where it had carved a two-inch-deep channel over the centuries. I looked back to find the source, but it seemed to appear from nowhere. "Probably coming from a tunnel nearby that we haven't discovered yet," Sonia said when I asked her about it.

We followed the stream as it flowed on the slight downward slope, and the tunnel started to twist and turn wildly for a few hundred feet. Several of the turns were sharp, and the space we had to shove through was tight. Sonia was small enough to crouch down and go through the wider portion at to bottom of the turns. Padraig tried to copy her, but still had to navigate spaces where his head seemed to be crushed between the rocks.

Nyk and I didn't even try to crouch, just pushing through as well as we could. It took half an hour to traverse that couple of hundred feet, but once we were past Sonia brought us to a halt. We all crouched down, and she spoke in a near whisper.

"The cave where your fugitive is located is straight down this tunnel. Go about two hundred feet, and it opens up on your left into a wide chamber."

Nyk thanked her for guiding us that far, and Padraig added his thanks for searching the cave system. I thanked her for waiting to lead us out again, getting a smile and pat on the shoulder as I passed.

We were moving more slowly now, careful not to kick any loose stones that might alert Surtr to our approach. Padraig halted halfway to where Sonia told us the chamber would be, waving Nyk and I in for a quick conference.

"Jack, I want you in the lead. Use the talisman, see what you can detect ahead. If Surtr happens to see you, he might hesitate for a few crucial seconds. He'd attack me immediately if I were spotted."

I wasn't a fan of throwing myself into danger, but he made a good point. Both of them followed a few steps behind me, the tunnel wide enough for them to walk side-by-side. It took another couple of minutes before I saw a dark spot ahead that I thought could be the entrance to the cavern. I held up a hand and waved for the others to stay behind as I crept closer.

Reaching up to touch the coin, I felt myself snap into the supernatural world with the sudden swiftness that seemed to be the new normal. The rock around me didn't fade as much as my office or the apartment complex had, so that I could still carefully move toward the opening. I could see a light now where there had been darkness before. Yellowish red, flickering like a campfire though I knew it would be foolish to have such a thing this deep in the earth.

As I got closer, I put my back against the rock and inched forward until I could see the thinnest portion of the cavern. The walls reflected the light back at me, brightly enough that I would have been blinded if it had been real. This was the essence of the jotunn, a beacon that must have drawn the Nine back in the days of the Vikings and the old gods.

"No need to creep around," a deep voice said suddenly. "Come, join me."

20

I hesitated, hoping that the jotunn was speaking from paranoia. When I inched forward a bit more, however, I found him sitting in the middle of the cavern, facing me and holding out a hand in invitation to join him. A small lantern sat on the ground beside him, the flame low as if he knew it wouldn't be needed for me to see him.

Surtr was nothing like I'd expected. Even seeing through his human mask, he was small and slight. His skin was pale but covered in soot or ash as if he spent most of his life around fires. Dark hair was tied back, hanging down past his shoulders. His beard was a wild tangle, thick and somehow darker than his hair. His teeth were a startling white when he spoke again.

"Join me. I mean you no harm, though you travel with a man I must kill."

I gulped but knew there was no point in skulking around any longer. I stood straight as I crossed the large chamber, sitting on a smooth stone that faced him. That's when I saw the sword laying on the ground at his feet, the blade alight with blue flames. It was close enough that I should have felt the heat on my face, but there was nothing more than the humid warmth of the caves.

"You're Surtr," I said, wanting him to know that I was aware of his identity.

"I am," he said proudly, seeming to sit up and push his shoulders back with pride. "Forty eighth of that name, guardian of Muspelheim."

"Sorry, I don't know where that is." It was the only thing I could think to say, my eyes drawn back to the sword at his feet. A sword that looked larger than I was and also no longer than a dagger. It made my brain hurt to look at it, and yet I couldn't tear my gaze away.

Surtr laughed, a sound that was likes stones grinding together as they rolled down a steep hill. "It is the world of fire, the forge of creation and the flames that shall end everything."

"That doesn't sound like a place I want to visit anytime soon."

He laughed again. "And who are you, besides a man who carries one of the Nine?"

"My name is Jack Dahlish," I said, my hand reaching up to touch the coin. "I'm here with Padraig Reilly, who has been tracking you since Dublin."

His face closed in, all amusement fading away. The tips of his beard almost seemed to curl in. "Yes, I know of whom you speak. He has much to answer for, Jack Dahlish. Why do you protect one such as he?"

"Protect? I'm just here to help him stop you. Too many people have died."

"Indeed." The smile returned to his face, below puzzled eyes. "You think it was my hand that has slain so many innocents?"

"Padraig knows it was you, Surtr. He didn't witness it, but we have ways of knowing when Nox have been around crimes, and your trail was at every one of them."

"It was," he said simply. "Because I was chasing the man who killed them."

"Huh?" Yeah, pithy response. I was feeling very confused in that moment. The sword kept trying to draw my attention, and every time I looked away from it, I had to focus for a few seconds before I remembered what was going on around me. I don't know what kind of magic was trapped in that blade, but I wasn't sure I ever wanted to see it in Surtr's hand.

"I did not kill those people, Jack Dahlish. I tried to protect them. I left my home in Iceland after I heard stories from my folk about a man who came among them and killed without remorse. A man who held a grudge against our kind, and no longer thought we deserved to be treated as more than vermin to be eliminated."

I realized that the folk he was talking about were other Nox. I'd often heard them refer to their various types in that overarching way, as if they were a large family that had grown apart. It was one of the things I sometimes envied about the supernatural creatures.

"Wait, you were chasing someone killing Nox? Then why were you around humans that had been killed?"

"Who said they were humans?"

Remember when I said my brain was moving slow? Yeah, I'm going to blame that for not realizing until that moment that I hadn't bothered to ask. Good or bad, I had just assumed humans were being killed when Padraig told me a jotunn was responsible. I hadn't even bothered to run simple internet searches to try and get information on the murders.

"So, you're saying Nox were being killed all across Europe and Asia, and now in North America?"

"Yes, Jack Dahlish. Many of my folk have been butchered. Men and women who lived good lives, children who were still innocent of the world around them. The man I chase has much of our blood on his hands, many crimes to answer for."

I didn't like where this was heading. "What about Hyderabad? Why attack two of the Nine, killing the humans with them?"

"Because the man you call Padraig had convinced the talisman bearer of that city that I was to blame. I tried to speak with her, as I'm speaking with you, but she would not listen. They attacked me, and I had no choice but to defend myself. I mourn for the lives I had to take that day, but I did not walk away unscathed." He waved at his chest, where I could see a vivid red scar in the gap where the top buttons of his shirt were undone. It wasn't a new scar, but still healing into the white line that he would bear for the rest of his life.

"Padraig? Why would one of us attack Nox? They must have been doing something to draw his attention. Attacking humans, maybe."

"What the bloody hell are you doing?" The voice screeched out the question behind me, and I turned to see the Irishman stomping into the cavern. Nyk was at his back, his eyes questioning as he looked at me calmly sitting across from the jotunn. He would see us by the dim light of the lantern, wondering why

I was chatting with this stranger we'd come to capture in the near darkness.

With my vision still in the supernatural world, I could see Padraig more clearly than ever. The chain and coin around his neck stood out sharply, shining through his clothing and thick caving suit. The rest of his body was covered in roiling black mist, almost writhing over his skin with only his face exposed. I could sense the power within him and wondered how I hadn't noticed it before.

"I didn't send you in here to listen to his tales, Dahlish. Attack him. Now!" Padraig held up his arm, and I saw a blade extending from his hand as he pointed at Surtr. The small sword was awash with the darkness that surrounded him, tendrils of it shooting out and retracting when they found nothing to cling to.

"Nyk, get away from him," I yelled as I rose to my feet and spun to face the Irishman. The bounty hunter acted quickly, trusting me without even asking why. Padraig whirled, his blade swinging through air the big man had occupied only second before. "What the hell are you?" I asked.

"He is Conand," Surtr said behind me, his voice calm and unhurried. I glanced back, surprised to see that the jotunn hadn't moved. "His kind are called fomorians, creatures that feed on the darkest of human emotions. They thrive on hate, despair, and desperation. There are few that remain, and humanity should be thankful for it."

"I never should have depended on you," Padraig spat out. Or Conand. I wasn't sure what to think, or who to trust. "You're weak, Dahlish, letting this creature bend your mind to his will.

This is how he killed so many people, by making them think he could be trusted."

Surtr moved at last, grasping his flaming sword and rising slowly to his feet. As he stood, he seemed to expand until his head brushed the roof of the cavern a few feet above my own. I understood now why the jotunn were feared as giants in the old myths. "Your own arrogance has betrayed you, Conand. Did you truly believe you could corrupt another of the Nine to do your dirty work?" He looked over to me, a gentle smile on his craggy face. "This one has much power within him, and he is only now beginning to realize it."

"Enough talk," the Irishman screamed. "We must fight him, Dahlish, or he'll kill more people. Here, in your city, where you're supposed to be their protector."

I looked between them, one a creature of flame and light and the other a creature of aggressive darkness and anger. It was impossible to tell from that which was telling the truth, despite the Hollywood stories of the man in black always being evil. I'd seen too many Nox with bad reputations turn out to be the best of people. Those like Mariah Mathis.

"Jack," Nyk called out from just outside the cavern, the light from his headlamp shining on the cave walls as he looked in. "What are we doing here?"

I hesitated, unsure what to say. Conand and Surtr faced off across the boulder that separated them, and their hatred for each other was almost palpable even without the talisman's ability to penetrate into the supernatural world. I reached up to touch the coin, and the moment my fingers came in contact through my clothing I felt a pulsing energy shoot through my body.

The talisman hanging around Conand's neck pulsed with the same rhythm, and he cried out in pain. The chain around his neck, the links that looked so delicate and yet had once withstood the force of a troll trying to rip it from me, seemed to just give way. The coin fell to the floor, landing with a heavy thud that echoed in the chamber loudly enough to make my head pound.

That was all I needed to see. "Padraig. Conand. Whatever your name is, drop the sword. I don't know exactly what you've done, but I'm certain you're involved in those deaths you claimed to be following."

The Irishman screamed incoherently, turning and running toward me as he pulled the dark sword back over his shoulder. I was unable to move, like a deer in headlights, as I saw the blade reverse course. It was slicing the air, aimed for my neck, and I felt like I was moving through viscous water as I raised an arm to try and block the blow.

A flaming sword slid in front of me, blocking the shadow-wrapped blade with a ringing clang. A large hand shoved me, almost gently, and sent me stumbling away from the two Nox as they snarled at each other over their weapons.

"What the hell is going on, Jack?" Nyk breathed in my ear as he caught me and held me steady.

"Uh, two giants are doing battle," I said lamely.

The swords swung through the air, clashing together with a ringing sound that echoed through my head. Sparks flew at each strike, and the shadows and flames appeared to be engulfing each other in the bare second before the blades were pulled back for another blow.

The two Nox were moving in a weaving circle, Conand pushing Surtr back a step with each blow. His anger and hatred were feeding his powerful strikes, and the shadow blade whipped through the air with a power that seemed unstoppable. And yet, Surtr met each blow with a strength that reminded me of mountains that stood against all the fury nature threw at them through thousands of years.

They neared the waterfall, no more than a steady trickle of water falling from a narrow crevice high up. It flowed across the lumps and bumps of the cavern wall, falling into a narrow channel that cut through the floor. I saw Surtr take a step back, his heel dropping into that hole and throwing him off balance. Conand pounced on the weakness, slamming his blade against the flaming sword and leaning in with all of his strength. The jotunn was pushed down onto a knee.

Surtr was pressing with all his might against the dark blade, the flames from his own weapon engulfing and then being engulfed by the shadows from his opponent's. "Why?" the jotunn asked through gritted teeth. "Why would you kill so many of our own kind?"

Conand's lips pulled back in a rictus grin. "Why the bloody hell not? They weren't doing me any good." He suddenly pushed harder against his foe, the shadows seeming to leap off his body and jump across to burn out in the flames that limned Surtr's body. Flames that dimmed a tiny bit with each shadow that disappeared.

"What about the man who wore the talisman before you stole it from his corpse? Why kill him?"

My head jerked over to look at the coin still laying where it had fallen from around the fomorian's neck. Stolen from the true holder, apparently. I walked over to look down on it, barely hearing the gloating response.

"The good Padraig Reilly. Such a foolish child, believing that I knew who had killed that poor family and their four brats. You should have seen his face when my blade took his life. Such sweet betrayal."

The coin laying on the ground seemed to be looking back at me. I almost felt that the face in gold profile was staring at me from the corner of his eye. Before I realized it, I was kneeling down with my hand only inches away. I stopped, wondering what would happen if I touched a coin not meant for me. I'd seen what happened to the few Nox who tried to take my own talisman, and it was not a pretty sight. How had the fomorian carried it for so long?

"I knew you were close," Conand continued, still straining against the jotunn. "So I took his little necklace, and I took his face. Then I buried the fool in a bog, where he'll never be found in our lifetimes."

"And you led me to Hyderabad, where you managed to convince a good woman to fight against me." Surtr's voice was sounding hoarse as he continued to put his full strength into holding back the dark sword that inched closer.

I could feel it in my fingers, the pulsing from the coin. Strangely, my own talisman started to beat faster as the energy from it flowed down my arm and into my fingertips. Working spit into my parched mouth, I realized there was only one choice in this moment. My fingers closed around the coin.

"Another gullible child," Conand said. "The woman thought I was so brave to have chased a mighty jotunn so far. Never thought to check if I was who I said I was. She would have given her life for me, and very nearly did."

"Only because you stabbed her in the back," Surtr said.

"Kept you occupied, didn't it?" Conand gloated. "Those flames of yours got too close when you jumped at me from the top of those crates. Surprised me, that. I knew I couldn't fight you with that wound, and I had to get away."

The pulsing stopped the moment I held the coin. Everything seemed to stop, even the water flowing through the cavern. *Use it!* The voice echoed through my head, and with a flash I knew what I had to do.

Surtr shouted in defiance as the shadows from the fomorian's blade began to extinguish the flames of his sword. It was a sound filled with rage, pain, and despair, and I knew it was feeding Conand and making him stronger. I turned back to the battle, seeing the opponents separated by no more than inches now, one grinning in triumph and the other wide-eyed with shocked realization. Even as I watched, the shadows writhing around Conand began to flow across the jotunn, starting at his hands and working their way up his arms.

"No," I said, quietly. I raised the coin in my hand, holding it out toward the two Nox and closing my eyes. I could feel the power of both talismans flowing through me, the chaos energy twining together. In moments, there was more of it than I could bear to hold within me. I released the power as I released my pent-up breath, opening my eyes to watch a bolt of brilliant blue light shoot across the cavern and slam into Conand's back.

The fomorian shrieked with pain, and Surtr was able to take advantage and push his opponent away. The jotunn's fire slowly returned as he shakily regained his feet, the shadows being burned away as he raised the flaming sword. "Conand of the Fomor, you have committed atrocities against our folk. For this, you face the ultimate punishment."

The Irishman was writhing against the energy still encircling his body, but he started to raise his dark blade as the flaming sword whistled through the air. He was too slow, and the bright flames tore through shadows and flesh alike. The cavern with filled with a high-pitched shriek. I clapped my hands over my ears as I ducked my head and squeezed my eyes shut.

When I opened them again, there was no sign of Conand. Surtr was standing tiredly, leaning with all his weight on his sword. He'd returned to his normal height, with only a dim light emanating from his body. I turned to look at Nyk, finding the bounty hunter leaning against the cavern wall with furrowed brows. In that moment, I wondered how the battle had looked to one without the ability to see the supernatural world.

"Jack Dahlish, you have done me a great service this day." Surtr took a few painful steps forward, then dipped into a bow. "I owe you a debt I fear I can never repay."

"It had to be done," I said, opening my hand to look at the coin that had been clenched in my fist. "I can't believe I didn't see him for what he was the moment I found him in my office."

The jotunn tilted his head, looking at me with searching eyes. "You were not the only one tricked by Conand's lies. I think that you will see more clearly in future. You will not be so easily fooled." He slumped down onto the rock he'd been sitting on when I first saw him, dropping the sword to the ground at his feet as he leaned tiredly on his knees. "I must rest here, but then I will return to my home. I have been gone for too long."

"Iceland?" I asked, remembering him mentioning it earlier. "Do you need anything? I can get you a plane ticket."

"Thank you, Jack Dahlish, but I shall make my own way. If you are ever in Iceland, look for a place in Reykjavik called The Crone's Corner. Ask for me there, and they will let me know." His eyes met mine. In that moment, I felt as if he could see every question I wanted to sit and ask. The jotunn only smiled and raised a hand. "Now, you must go. There is other danger in your city, and time is growing short. You can still prevent another death."

I wondered how he knew anything about that, living in this dim cavern for the last week or more. But he was right, I didn't have time to linger. Something inside was urging me to go back, compelling me to get to San Antonio before it was too late.

Nyk was staring at the ground and shaking his head in confusion as I approached. He looked up as I put a hand on his arm. "What just happened, Jack? I thought I saw two giants, one with a sword of light and the other with a sword of darkness. But then I'd blink, and it would be no more than two men grappling against each other."

"It's the air," I said. "Not enough oxygen this deep, probably."

"Yeah, maybe that's it."

"Come on, Nyk. Time for us to get back to Sonia and return to the real world."

He looked around. "What about Padraig? Is he coming?"

"He already left," I assured him, leading him out of the cavern and into the tunnel that felt like I had left it years before.

21

S onia was confused when only two of us returned, but I told her Padraig was staying with our fugitive until more help could be sent down. Nyk gave me a questioning look, but thankfully neither of them pursued it further. I like to think I was just that persuasive, but I had a feeling that the two coins I carried might have had something to do with it.

It took an hour and a half to get out of the caves, and I can't remember the last time I enjoyed breathing in fresh cold air more. Air that quickly set me to shivering after so long in the warmth of the caves. Even with the thick protective suit on, I could feel my skin prickling.

Back at Nyk's truck, we silently peeled out of the suits and packed the gear into the plastic crates that it had come from. Sonia kept looking at me strangely, and I felt certain she was wondering why we would leave only one person to guard a supposedly dangerous fugitive. The bounty hunter saw the direction of my focus and gave me a gentle nudge and nod. I felt better knowing he would handle things, even if it meant I'd have to do some explaining of my own to him later on.

"Thank you for guiding us in," I told Sonia, once I was wrapped in my herringbone coat again. "We owe you a debt."

She only grunted in assent, her face tight with thought. I raised a hand to Nyk, then slid into my car. Fatigue was setting in after the strenuous journey underground, along with witnessing the battle between the two powerful Nox, and I almost closed my eyes to try and make the burning stop. But I knew if I did that, it could be hours before they opened again. Instead, I pushed the button to start my engine, pressed the switch to activate the seat warmers, and drove away from the graveled lot.

I still didn't have a return call from Karen, or any voice or text messages. That kicked off my worries again, even as the most recent events kept replaying in my mind. I was also questioning the certainty I had felt earlier in the day. Well, yesterday according to the clock on my dash that told me we'd been in the caves for more longer than I'd expected. Just because Barbara hung around to ask questions about me didn't mean she was some kind of killer. Or even a Nox.

My thoughts were fuzzy as I drove, trying to remember why I'd seemed so certain that I knew who was draining those poor men after talking to the restaurant employees. I raised a hand to my pounding head, sucking in breath as I touched the tender skin where I'd banged it against the stalactite. I'd forgotten all about that with the craziness that happened after, but now I pulled down my visor and opened the illuminated mirror to get a look. My forehead was already a sickly yellow, and I knew I'd be wearing a hat to hide the bruise for several days.

Traffic was light after midnight, so I was running on cruise control in the middle lane of the interstate. That gave my mind time to wander where it would, needing only a small amount of focus for my driving. Wherever it went, time seemed hazy for a while. I barely remember most of the trip, until a familiar building drew my eye and I realized I was exiting the freeway onto streets that would take me home.

The only thing I wanted in that moment was my bed. Even after fifteen hours of rest the night before, my energy was expended, and the reserves were almost empty. When I pulled into my driveway, I didn't even bother trying to pull under the narrow carport. I just tumbled out of the vehicle and dragged myself to the front door. My key seemed to fight me as I shoved it into the lock, until finally sliding smoothly in and turning with a click.

I shut the door behind me as I stepped into my small foyer, shrugging out of my coat and putting it on one of the hooks. The talisman Conand had stolen from the true holder in Ireland was in a pocket of it. I had a momentary thought that I should put it somewhere safe, but the only place I knew was the steel-walled closet in my office, and I was too exhausted to make that trip. It would be fine where it was for a night.

Dragging steps took me through the dark living room and into the kitchen. I pulled the fridge door open, grabbed one of the bottled waters I kept for guests who didn't like tap water, and chugged it down. I hadn't realized how parched I was until then, and I grabbed a second bottle before closing the door to shut off the light from within.

Leaning back against the scratched old countertop, I drank the second bottle more slowly. My lips felt dry, my eyes burned even worse, and my muscles felt like they were going to refuse to work for several days. A voice in the back of my mind said I was going to be sore as hell the next day and reminded me to take a Tylenol before bed. Then I stared at the cabinet where I kept my pill bottles for a few minutes before I worked up the energy to take the two steps and pull it open. I shook a couple of the white tablets into my palm, and then tossed them back with a drink of water.

I filled the now empty bottle from the sink, carrying it with me into the bedroom, which was shrouded in darkness, with heavy curtains over the windows to keep out any sunlight for the rare days when I slept in. My arms felt like lead weights, so I didn't bother with flipping on a light. I set the water bottle on my bedside table, feeling with my fingers to make sure it wasn't too close to the edge. Then I turned and padded into the bathroom, pulling my clothes off as I went.

My shoes were easily kicked into a corner, and my shirt soon followed. The jeans gave me a little difficulty, and I wobbled as I stood on one foot to pull the pants off each leg, pulling my boxers off at the same time. Socks were a bigger struggle, and I almost ended up on the floor as I took the first off. Once all my clothing was shed, I left it in a pile on the floor and felt around the bathroom until I found the handle for the shower.

As the water ran and I waited for it to heat up, I looked toward the spot I had long ago plugged in a night light. It was fairly old, but I hadn't expected it to burn out without any warning. Yet it was completely dark, while the one in the kitchen had provided a faint illumination. Shrugging, I decided to worry about it in the morning. After almost ten years in the house, I knew it well enough to navigate without seeing a thing.

The hot water flowing from the shower head soothed my increasingly complaining muscles and washed away all the dirt and grit I'd picked up crawling through several miles of caves. Once I was clean, I leaned my head against an arm on the tiled wall and just let the water flow over my skin. When I realized I was starting to fall asleep, I forced myself to shut off the water and reach out for a towel.

I dried off quickly, goosebumps covering my arms and legs in the cold air. After rubbing the towel through my hair to make sure it was dry, I tossed it back over the bar and stepped out onto the cold tile floor. I took quick steps back onto the slightly less cold wood floors of my bedroom, and then felt my way across to my bed. My covers were thrown back, just as I'd left them when I jumped out of bed the morning before. I slid under them, pulling the sheet and comforter up under my chin and waiting for my body heat to warm them up.

My eyes were closed, my breathing beginning to slow, and my brain was already in that wild half-sleep state where thoughts turn into wild imaginings.

Then the voice snapped me awake.

"It's about time you came home, Jack."

22

I scrambled to pull my arms out from under the covers, reaching over to tug the chain that turned on my bedside lamp. It was a low wattage bulb, just enough for me to see words on pages when I read a book before falling asleep, but it gave me enough light to see the woman lying on her side near me.

"Barbara? What the hell are you doing in my house? What are you doing in my *bed*?"

She smiled languidly, a sultry look in her eyes. "I figured it was time for us to get better acquainted. After all, I need to know everything about you if I'm going to approve of you dating my sister."

I jumped out of the bed, then realized I was naked and grabbed a pillow to hold it in front of my groin. "Is this how you get to know her boyfriends? Breaking into their homes and crawling into their beds?"

"You'd be surprised how well that works," she purred, running a hand along her side. I noticed for the first time what she was wearing, or more importantly not wearing. Karen's sister was in my bed in just bra and panties, with thigh-high stockings to boot.

"This isn't right," I said, hopefully sounding as indignant as I felt. "Get out of here! If you want to talk to me, we can meet later today. Somewhere public, with lots of people."

Barbara didn't move, except to keep stroking her tanned skin. Too much of which I could see. "What's wrong, Jack? Don't I look pretty? Wouldn't you like to lie beside me while I run my hands through your hair? Would you like to let my lips caress your skin?"

"Holy hells," I said. I really did want that, but what heterosexual male wouldn't feel that same desire while looking at the lovely brunette lying so temptingly in their bed? But there was no way I'd ever do more than fantasize about it. "I'm in love with your sister, Barbara. She's the only one I want to share my bed with."

She pouted, her lips plumping out as her brows drew together. "You're hurting my feelings, Jack. Aren't I just as beautiful as my sister? Just as desirable?"

"Yes, you are. You'll make some guy really happy one day, but it won't be me. And it definitely won't be here." I retreated to my pile of clothes and bent to grab my boxers. It was a struggle to pull them on under the pillow. Then I threw the dirty t-shirt on over my head, feeling better now that I wasn't so exposed.

Barbara rolled onto her hands and knees, crawling slowly across the bed. Her eyes were locked on mine as she smiled. Her voice had dropped several octaves, becoming slow and seductive. "Come on, Jack. No one ever needs to know what happens here. It's just a few hours of fun, and I can tell that you need it as badly as I do."

"I do need it," I groaned, and took a step forward before I shook my head. "I need it from Karen, not from you. *Karen* is the woman I want to be with." I winced, realizing it sounded like I was trying to convince myself of that fact more than I was asserting it to Barbara.

She stepped from the bed, one slim foot after the other. Standing there, she raised her arms in a sinuous stretch, presenting her body to me in its full glory. I had to blink, forcing myself to look away, and found my eyes straying back to the black lace that covered the parts of her body I suddenly ached to see. To touch.

"How long has it been, Jack?" she asked in a low voice. "I know my sister, and she hasn't given you any physical satisfaction yet. I can, Jack. Let me show you just how much pleasure you're missing out on."

I wasn't sure how it happened, but suddenly I was standing only inches away as Barbara ran her hands over my chest. I opened my mouth, trying to force out words that would make her stop. Her hands slid under my t-shirt, and it felt like electricity crackled where her fingertips met my skin. I looked at my arms as they raised up to allow her to pull the shirt off, feeling betrayed by them.

"That's it, just relax and enjoy. I'm going to give you an experience like you've never felt before."

A croak came from my throat, the only thing I could get out as I tried to yell at her to stop touching me. To let me go and get out of my house. My head felt so fuzzy and wrong, the way it did when I'd had to take Valium as a teenager before having my wisdom teeth removed.

"Yes, just relax." Barbara turned us around, and then pushed me back to fall onto the bed. I tried to make my body roll away, unable to do so as she crawled up to kneel over me.

Her fingers ran through my hair, and I closed my eyes trying to pretend it was Karen. "No!" she said, slapping my cheek. "You are with *me*, Jack. *I* am the one giving you pleasure, not my sister."

How could she have known what I was thinking? I tried to figure it out, but my thoughts grew fuzzy once more as her slender fingers began to rub over my scalp again. I couldn't focus on anything but her. Our eyes locked together, our skin touching.

"I wasn't going to do this," Barbara said quietly, almost as if speaking to herself. "I was going to leave you alone, but then you turned my sister against me."

Her fingers grabbed my hair, twisting and pulling painfully. I felt ashamed that it only aroused me more, grateful for any attention this beautiful creature would deign to give me.

"Karen told me I had to leave, that I couldn't stay with her another night. Because of you, and because of *this*." Her long black nails scratched down my chest, drawing lines of blood as she outlined the talisman still around my neck. She sneered at it, raising her hand to tap it aside disdainfully.

The moment she touched the coin, the clouds in my head cleared instantly. At the same time, my vision snapped over into the supernatural world and I drew in a sharp breath as I looked at the creature straddling my stomach.

Her skin was dark red, almost black. It looked dry and cracked, as rough as her human mask had been soft. The ears on either side of her narrow head were long with tips that looked sharp enough to cut skin. Her eyes were slitted, yellow cat's eyes that seemed to stare deep into my soul. There was no hair on her head, just skin stretched tight over her skull.

Barbara felt the change in my attitude, the stiffening of my body as I looked on her true form. She hissed at me, and a long red tongue slithered out between sharp teeth. It was covered in short spikes, like those found in the first two victims. I knew that if I could have called Mariah at that moment, she would confirm having found one in the waiter, as well.

"Get off me, you bitch!" I shouted as I reached up to push her away. Her skin felt wrong under my hands, like it was only loosely attached to the muscle below it. I couldn't seem to get the purchase I needed to lever her body off mine. She only hissed out laughter, leaning closer.

"Give me a kiss, Jack. I promise you won't feel a thing." The spiked tongue slithered out as I put my hands on her shoulders, pushing against her as she tried to get close enough to touch me with it. My eyes focused on one of the barbs, and I could see a small drop of moisture on the end that looked like venom.

"You seduced them," I said in realization. "Then, when you got close enough, you used one of those things to... what? Put them to sleep?"

The tongue drew back into her mouth. "What would be the fun in that? It only makes you more compliant, willing to do anything I ask of you. Willing to endure whatever it takes to be near me.

"Those men were so easy, Jack. Lonely. Horny. I showed them a little interest, and that was all it took to be invited into their homes. We had our 'dates', and they told me all about their troubles over a meal. The widower, searching for someone to fill the void in his life. The bachelor, convinced that he could never love again after his heart was broken.

"But the last one, Jack, he was the hardest. The waiter, who stayed loyal to you and my sister until the last. He gave me bits and pieces, when I wanted everything. I *demanded* everything. And I took it."

She was pushing harder now, and it required all of my quickly draining strength to keep her back. If I hadn't been through the caves, maybe I could have fought her off easily. But then, if she hadn't touched the coin I would have been under her spell while she drained my life away like the other poor men she'd killed.

"Why do you hate her so much?" I asked through gritted teeth.

"Who? My sister? The perfect little princess? She was the one my parents loved, the one who followed all their stupid rules. Do you know what it's like to be constantly hungry, Jack? To be on the brink of starvation every moment of every agonizing day, and then be told that you can't give in and take what you need?" She lunged suddenly, and almost got close enough for her darting tongue to touch my face as I rolled my head away desperately.

Barbara hissed in frustrated disappointment. "Karen was the one the boys always wanted to be with. She would date them, and the moment it started to get serious she'd go running to mother to cry about how she didn't know if she could trust herself to remain in control around them. Sniveling little bitch."

I swallowed, trying to get rid of the lump that had formed in my throat. So much for my hope that Karen or Barbara might have been adopted, that I didn't need to worry about my girlfriend being a Nox.

It made sense. The way I'd always been so compelled to open up with her, and the way she'd so easily accepted my story about the Filii Nox and the talisman that let me see them for what they truly were.

"I decided that if she won't take what they're offering, then why shouldn't I do it for her?" Barbara grinned, a gruesome sight with her sharp teeth spaced widely enough for me to see the red tongue writing behind them like a caged beast. "At first, I thought they might not want to be with me. But do you know how many of them resisted when I offered myself to them, Jack?"

"At least one," I grunted, feeling my shoulders starting to refuse the effort I need to hold her back.

"None of them ever resisted. They willingly came to me, begging me to touch them and give them the pleasure my sister never would. They called out *my* name in ecstasy, not hers." She closed her eyes, leaning her head back as if enjoying each of them again in her memory. "They gave their lives to *me*, not Karen."

"Heartless bitch," I said through gritted teeth. I looked around, hoping to find something I could use as a weapon against her. The talisman was still cold and lifeless against my chest, and I tried to mentally will it to produce the heat and light as it had when I was attacked the same day it went around my neck.

"I think you might be the one that finally breaks Kare Bear. She really does love you, for some reason. Just a human," she spat out in disgust. "When she finds out that I took you from her before I left town, she'll never recover. We'll see who's the perfect little princess then."

Barbara lunged forward again, and my hands slipped against her rough, leathery skin. My palms were slick with sweat, and I had to quickly throw my elbows up to keep my forearms pushing against the Nox as she hissed in triumph. The long tongue darted out, only an inch away from my skin as I pushed my head back into the cushioned mattress and promised to send a thank you card to the salesman who talked me out of a firmer model.

She began to jerk against me, trying to push down further. I could feel her sliding against my arms, the sweat-slick skin not giving me the grasp I needed to keep her at bay for much longer. I knew I was about to die, and I couldn't count on Ollie to come through the door and save me this time.

I closed my eyes, seeing Karen's face behind my eyelids. Her smile, the way her nose scrunched up when she found something especially funny. I felt my fingers running through her hair, the coolness of her cheek when I cupped it in my hand as I leaned in to kiss her. I heard her laugh, tasted her breath when our lips met. I felt the joy that always surged within me when I saw her face across a room, or when I caught a whiff of perfume that made me think of her. And in that moment, I knew that no matter what she was, I would always love Karen Kilgraff.

Barbara screamed in pain, throwing herself back from the bed. As I looked up in shock, I saw her standing in the doorway of the bathroom. Two long streaks of scarred flesh ran down her chest, where my arms had been holding her back only seconds earlier. "No, that's not possible. It can't be."

Love. That's what her weakness was, the reason she targeted men who were alone. I sat up on the bed, supporting myself on shaking arms as she stared at me in horrified anger. "I told you, Barbara. I love Karen, and I always will."

"But you know what she is now. You know that she's like me." She waved her hands along her body as she said it.

"That doesn't matter. Her beauty attracted me in the beginning, but it's not even a tenth of what draws me to your sister. Her kindness, her goodness... those are the things that thrill me and make me ache to be with her every waking moment."

Barbara hissed, drawing her lips back in a snarl that seemed to take up half her long face. "I will still have you, Jack. Men are fickle beasts, always drawn to something new, thinking it will be better than what they already have. The moment your thoughts stray, I'll be there to take everything from you."

"No, you won't." I sighed, reaching up to touch the talisman against my chest and feeling a thrum of energy pulse through my fingers. "How many have you killed, Barbara? How many men have you drained to satisfy the hunger you won't control?"

She laughed, a gloating sound. "Why only men? Women taste just as sweet. But you're right, I do so enjoy taking the life from men. Vile creatures, who pretend to love only until they get what they want. Until they dip their filthy penises."

I wondered who had hurt this woman so much that she turned against all men. I'd seen it before, men and women who got sick of being treated poorly, who were cheated on one too many times and could no longer trust another. It pained me to see such hatred in her, this woman who could have one day been as close as my own sister.

"Especially this time of year," she said, staring to slowly circle around me as I stood my ground against the bed. "Valentine's Day. As if naming a single day makes it okay to express love and then forget about it. Do you know how many people suffer heartbreak in the week after this foolish holiday? More than I've ever killed, I can tell you that."

That reminded me that it was now Sunday. The day I'd been looking forward to all week, with the plans I'd made for the special date with Karen. I realized I had been selfishly hoping that taking her to dinner and presenting her with flowers would have ended with us both sharing the bed I had only barely escaped alive minutes earlier. It made me feel dirty to think about that now.

"Too many," I said. "I can't let you kill again, Barbara. It has to end now."

"What will you do, Jack? Are you going to kill *me*?" She smirked at the words. "That would hurt my sister almost as much as me killing you. The foolish girl still thinks I can be saved."

I grinned, feeling a lightening of my spirit. Killing her had been the only thing I could think of, and I'd known how much pain it would bring to Karen as well as myself. It wasn't something I'd wanted to do, but I couldn't see any other way to stop her from killing more people. Then her words sparked an idea that felt right somehow.

My fingers traced the profile on the coin, a gold face set onto the silver disk with intricate workmanship. The pulse of energy flowed through my fingers again, and in that instant I knew how to do it. How to end the killings without having to kill the creature standing in front of me.

I wasn't even sure how I did it, but I pulled some of the Chaos energy from the talisman, drawing it into my hand. Amazingly, I felt a thread of it also coming from the coin that rested in a pocket of my coat hanging from the hook by the door. Barbara saw my expression change, and confusion flashed across her face. Her eyes darted around the room, and then she turned to run as my hand was lifting. Her steps were fast, and she escaped through the bedroom door.

Somehow, I felt myself split in twain. I was still standing by the bed, but I was also standing by the front door. Barbara saw me there, her eyes going wide with shock as she tried to stop her forward momentum. She was too late, as my hand raised to grasp the top of her head. The energy I'd pulled from the coins poured out of my fingers, flowing through her body as she screamed shrilly until there was no more breath to scream with.

We stood like that for several minutes, and I felt the changes as they happened. It was like washing an oil stain from the driveway, spraying the water until the dark slick flowed away to reveal the clean concrete underneath. Except that I was washing away her hunger, her hatred, her ability to kill.

Barbara slumped to the floor the moment my hand pulled back from her head. Her eyes were closed, but I could see her eyelids twitching as if she were deep in REM sleep. I blinked, seeing two rooms at the same time. Blinked again and was only looking at the bare walls of my bedroom. I had a moment to wonder what had just happened.

Then the world went dark.

23

A hand was touching my cheek when I woke up, warm skin against the prickly beard growth. I smiled, remembering a dream about Karen and thinking she must have come by to surprise me. There could be no better way to wake up than to open my eyes and see her radiant smile above me.

When I opened my eyes, I saw instead a different face, pale under long dark hair that fell to drape my head. "What did you do to me?" she asked hoarsely.

I blinked a few times, groaning as my pounding headache and the memories of what had happened flooded back. It was still dark in the room, lit only by the faint light from the lamp. There was a hammer tapping insistently inside my skull, sending waves of pain through my head. I reached up to wrap my hands around my face, trying to push the agony into the background.

"What did you do to me?" she asked again, quietly insistent.

"I don't know," I said through my hands. "I just wanted to make you better."

Barbara's hand pulled away, and I heard movement as she slumped against the wall. I'd somehow fallen onto the floor, lying between the bed and the doorway into the bathroom. I wondered if I'd hit my head, but I had a feeling the headache was from the way I'd somehow channeled the chaos energy from the talismans into my girlfriend's sister.

The sound of muffled sobs made me turn my head, sending shooting bursts of pain throbbing behind my eyes. Barbara was sitting against the wall, huddled with her knees pulled up and her arms wrapped around them. Even though she still wore only bra and panties, she no longer looked like a seductress. Instead, she was a waif, lost and alone in the world.

A surge of pity filled me, and I wondered if whatever I'd done was worse than killing her would have been. I tried to look at her with the power of the talisman, tried to see her true appearance, but nothing would happen. Maybe it was the headache, or maybe I'd drained the coin's power and it had to build back up.

Then I realized I could see a faint pink haze in the air, and my nose was filled with the smell of peach blossoms. I was still looking at the supernatural world, it was just that Barbara was no longer anything more than the human she appeared to be. Somehow, I had turned a Nox into a human. I wanted to be amazed, I wanted to think back and figure out how such a thing could even be possible, but the headache was getting worse and I couldn't bear to think at all.

The next thing I felt was a cool washcloth spread across my forehead. I'd blacked out again. I forced one eye open in a squint, looking up at Barbara. She held two white pills in one hand, a glass of water in the other. "Take these. They'll help with the headache."

I probably shouldn't have taken anything she gave me, but the pain was so bad I would have been happy to die at that moment. I popped the pills in my mouth, bit down to spread the bitter taste across my tongue, and then sipped water to wash it all down. There was a pillow under my head now, and I almost laughed when I realized it was probably the one I'd been hiding behind earlier.

The washcloth was taken away, and I heard water as it was dipped into a bowl and then splashes as she wrung it out before placing it over my forehead and eyes again. Her hands were gentle, her touch almost hesitant as she began to massage my temples and then the back of my neck at the base of my skull. Gradually, the pain started to recede until I could focus on something else again.

I sat up against the side of the bed. "Thanks," I said, giving her a wan smile of appreciation.

"No, Jack. Thank you." Barbara looked at me with wet eyes, and I could still see trails on her cheeks where the tears had fallen. "I... I can't believe all the things I've done. The hatred I've felt for so long. It's gone now, but I still have the guilt. That will never go away, will it?"

"I'm afraid it won't, but now you have the opportunity to do something to make up for it. Improve lives, instead of ending them."

She shook her head, her eyes on the ground between us. "I should be punished. You should have killed me."

I reached out, placing a finger under her chin to raise her eyes to my own. "Don't say that. No one *deserves* to die, no matter what they've done. I would turn you over to the police, let them lock you away, but we could never prove that it was you who killed those men. Whatever forensic clues you left behind won't tie to who you are now."

She grimaced, her eyes darting away. "How, then? How can I ever make up for what I've done?"

I heard the front door locks click back just before it was pushed open. "Barbara?" a tentative voice called out. The house was still dark aside from the lamp in the bedroom. I knew Karen would be coming toward us.

"You can apologize to your sister," I whispered. "That's a good start. Be the person she's always wanted you to be, the kind of woman who helps others instead of thinking only about what they should be doing for her."

Barbara nodded faintly, pushing herself to her feet and padding out of the bedroom. I heard Karen gasp, the surprise and tremulous fear in her voice. "Barbara? What are you doing here? Why aren't you wearing anything? What did you do?"

I heard a quiet reply, and then a muffled conversation as the sisters talked. Karen gasped loudly at several points, but for the most part she listened as her sister apologized for all the hurtful things she'd done over the years, and then confessed to all the men and women she'd killed.

I'm not sure how long I remained on the floor of my bedroom hearing snatches of their conversation. I closed my eyes again, wetting the cloth and draping it over my face as the headache pounded away behind my eyes. It felt like every hangover I'd ever had in my teens and twenties rolled into one horrible moment.

A hand touched my uncovered cheek, timidly making contact and then pulling away. I reached out to grab Karen's wrist, gently guiding her hand back to my cheek. "Oh, Jack. I don't know how you did it, but I'll never be able to thank you."

"You don't need to thank me, Karen. I could never hurt your sister. I love you too much for that."

"I love you, too." She leaned her forehead against mine, and I felt a tear fall against my cheek. "I am so sorry. For lying to you this whole time, for not telling you what I am."

"No," I said, raising a hand to her lips before she could go on. "You don't ever need to apologize to me. It doesn't matter what you are, it can't change the way I feel about you."

Her body shook, and I could feel the tremors through our contact. There was so much I wanted to say, but she already knew it all. Every word of it had been said between us in our actions over the last couple of months, and we knew each other as well as any two people could.

"I have to leave, Jack."

"I know."

"No. I mean I have to leave San Antonio. I need to be away from here while we figure out what to do with Barbara."

"I know," I said again. It was my turn to touch her cheek. I could feel the roughness of her skin, her true self. Somehow, without even having to force my senses open, I was still in both worlds. I knew that if I removed the cloth that covered my eyes, I'd see Karen as she truly was.

She knew it, too, and pressed her hands against either side of the wet cloth as she brought her lips to mine. This time, I knew why I suddenly felt a burst of energy once she broke the kiss. While Barbara had used her abilities to drain life and vitality, Karen used hers to give it.

With a whispered "I love you", she pulled back and I heard her footsteps as she returned to the kitchen. Barbara spoke to her, begging her to stay with me and not give up her life and love for a sister who had brought only pain. I could have told her to save her breath. Karen would never leave her sister to handle the consequences of her actions alone, any more than I could have killed Barbara and lived with myself afterward.

I heard the front door open, then gently close soon after. I knew I should get up since my headache had receded to a dull ache after Karen's kiss, but I lay there for a long time. It was the only way I could pretend that the wetness on my face came from the damp rag.

24

V isiting the Den was a new experience after Valentine's Day. As I sat on my customary stool, nursing a pale ale that Richard had just taken delivery of that morning, I had to keep glancing up at the other patrons for short stretches before averting my eyes.

Ever since that night, I no longer had to force myself into the supernatural world to capture short glimpses of what awaited there. I could see it all the time, the visage below the masks and the trails that filled the air around me. I could see the human world, as well, like a 3D movie where you could close each eye and see a different version of the image on the screen. It took a bit of concentration to separate the two, but I was becoming more adept as the days went by.

Nyk settled onto a stool nearby with a tired grunt, his shoulder almost rubbing against mine even though there was an empty seat between us. He sat there in silence, holding up a hand to get Richard's attention, and then wrapped his large hands around the cold glass when a drink arrived. The noise around us swelled and receded like a wave of sound, but we only drank and thought our thoughts.

"I know I've already said it, but thanks again for helping Surtr get out of the country."

"No problem, Jack. Once he explained what happened in that cavern, I was happy to help."

The jotunn had remained deep in the caves for two days after his confrontation with Conand, before navigating his way out again. Through a path that was a quarter as long as the one we'd traversed to find him. It had amazed Sonia when Nyk showed it to her. The entrance was so well hidden that it was only a hundred feet from a popular hiking trail and had never been discovered. Surtr showed up in my office that evening, the place I'd been spending most of my time lately, afraid to go home and relive the memories that besieged me there. Nyk helped me get him on an unregistered flight back to his home in Iceland.

"Sorry to hear about Karen," he rumbled lowly, his gaze resting on the far wall. I hadn't told anyone about what happened with Barbara, or about the sisters being Nox. But Karen's sudden sabbatical had been part of a twenty-four-hour cycle. An anchor and investigative reporter from the second biggest station in town stepping away for "family reasons" at the height of her popularity was big news at the other stations. Friends like Ollie and Nyk could see how hard I was taking things, and they naturally assumed that she had broken up with me.

"She has things that need to be handled," I said, rolling the half empty glass between my palms. "Things that are much more important than our relationship."

When I'd called Ollie around lunch on Valentine's Day and told him he didn't have to worry about finding more shriveled corpses, he wanted an explanation. I told him simply that the killer had been handled, and after a few more questions with no answers he was resigned to not knowing more. He'd worked with me long enough to know that if I was being so reticent, there was probably a lot of stuff in the background that he really didn't want to know.

He couldn't go to his bosses with such sparse information, knowing a reassurance of "it's taken care of" from a private investigator would have been worse than useless in their eyes. But he was able to relax, and when I saw them a few days later I could tell Annie had figured some of it out and wasn't expecting more desiccated bodies to turn up. She also frowned all the harder at me as we shared a lunch of fajita tacos.

For the first time, I glanced over at Nyk. I'd been afraid to do so since he sat on the stool, this first time we were together after that night in the caves. I was never sure exactly what I might see with my new vision. He looked the same as he always had, making me sigh with relief. Whatever Nox traces were left from his long-ago ancestor, they seemed to manifest only in his larger and more muscular frame.

Looking at Richard when I entered the bar had been my biggest shock. I'd known since meeting him that he was a human, so I'd expected him to look the same as he always had. But now, looking at him leaning over the bar to laugh with a customer as he took an empty glass, I could only shake my head in shock once more. He looked almost majestic, with an inner glow forming a sort of nimbus around him. There was a pulsing white light on his left shoulder, which had puzzled me until I realized it was his Relic. I wasn't sure if I'd be able to see all Relics now, or just whatever his might be. The talisman around my neck didn't look any different when I looked down, nor did the one still in the pocket of my coat where I'd carried it since Conand's defeat.

"Are you sure about this?" Nyk asked, dragging me from my thoughts and reminding me of the reason we were meeting at the Den.

"Very," I said. "I have to find someone to wear the coin that used to belong to the real Padraig Reilly." And the best place to start was with the only other member of the Nine I knew where to find. Gitna Sridhar lived and worked in Hyderabad, India. I hoped she had recovered from the coma she'd been in since the fight against the jotunn, but if not, then perhaps I could find a way to help her. "The world needs all of us working to keep it safe."

"Yeah, I suppose so." He drained his glass, holding it up until Richard looked over and noticed the need for a refill. "I remember the years before you took up one of the Nine, Jack. It wasn't the wild west or anything, but there was definitely some bad shit going on. If you can help to prevent that happening elsewhere, then I support it." He placed a large hand on my shoulder, squeezing almost painfully. "I'll take care of things while you're gone."

"You better," I said with a faint smile.

I hope you've enjoyed the third book in the Dahlish series. Jack will be back with a new adventure far from San Antonio.

In the meantime, read on for a short story about events that occur in San Antonio while he's gone. Old enemies return, and the Nox world gets a little more complicated.

Undefended

I opened the door, my hand on the knob as I stood on the threshold. The wooden desk was highlighted by the morning sun, with the expensive office chair behind it almost inviting me to sit. Two armless chairs were on this side of the desk, ready for clients to settle in as they poured out their problems, hoping they'd come to the right place to find a solution.

After a week, it still didn't feel right to be there without Jack. Through all the years I'd known him, from the days when he was a gawky neophyte still dipping his feet in the supernatural world, this had been his base of operations. His sanctum from the world that raged beyond these walls.

With a sigh, I entered the office and closed the door behind me with a gentleness that surprised so many who looked at my heavily muscled seven-foot frame. What they could never understand was that I'd been larger than everyone else almost from the moment I emerged into the world. As a kid, I'd had to learn to moderate my strength lest I destroy everything in our house.

I pulled the chair back from the desk, lowering myself with a contented sigh. Not even a creak of protest, as if the chair had been ordered specially to contain my bulk. I'd have to ask Jack where he'd gotten it when he returned.

If he returned.

He sent me an email to let me know he'd arrived safely in India, and I hadn't heard from him since. Jack Dahlish was a hard man for me to figure out at the best of times, but since Karen Kilgraff had departed San Antonio and left him broken-hearted, it had gotten even harder to read him.

The cop told me that Jack just needed space. That after a week or two, he'd get his head right and be ready to return to the city and get back to work. I hoped he was right. I wasn't cut out for investigative work.

My name is Nyk Walsh, and I'm a bounty hunter. If some scumbag cut and run before he got the justice he deserved, I was the man to call to bring him in. The supernatural Filii Nox would call me in when one of their own needed to be tracked down, especially if it was outside the territories covered by one of the Nine.

Jack was one of them, the people who wore special Relics that allowed them to somehow see the Nox through the human disguises they wore to blend in with the world. He'd tried to explain it to me once, something about smells and tastes, but it didn't make much sense. I was happy to stick to the signs I could see with my own eyes.

I opened the lid of Jack's laptop, using my pinky to type in the password he'd given me as he was boarding his plane. Several emails greeted me on the screen, all of them from people asking when Jack was going to return. He would never believe it, but the Nox of San Antonio had come to depend upon him a great deal in the ten years he'd been working to keep them safe.

The last email, less than an hour old, was a request for a meeting. *Walsh, need to meet. Urgent. I'll have a margarita waiting for you.*

There was no name, and the sender email address was some anonymous string of numbers and letters. But I knew almost instantly who had sent it. Someone that I'd thought was out of town for a long-term absence.

I cracked my knuckles as I closed the laptop lid and stood to leave the office. He'd better have a good reason for being back so soon, or I'd get to enjoy myself more than I expected when I woke up that morning.

*　*　*　*　*

The residential street was quiet, and I'd passed only one older woman walking the sidewalk with her arms pumping as she sped along. I parked at the curb opposite the house I was interested in, cutting the engine of my truck. Jack liked to joke that it was a monster truck, but it was just a dually that I'd had jacked up a bit to make travel on unpaved roads easier. A lot of work had gone into strengthening the frame of the truck, enough that I could ram almost any other vehicle and take little damage. That had come in handy more times than I could count through the years.

When I stepped down to the curb, I ran my eyes over the houses across the street. There was nothing out of the ordinary to be seen. At least, nothing I could see. I thought Jack would possibly pick up on something if he were here, some smell or taste that would tell him a vampire had driven by three weeks ago. He was useful like that.

I checked both ways before crossing the street. More than once as a kid, I'd darted across a road without looking. My dad had been incensed when a driver hit me in my preteen years, but I think he was mostly upset about the repair bill he'd ended up covering to keep the driver from talking about the kid who stood up with only a few scratched bruises after the hood was crumpled like the car had driven into a telephone pole.

The driveway I entered was empty. This house didn't have a garage, so I started to worry that I'd jumped to a wrong conclusion about who had sent the email. A pile of newspapers scattered in front of the door worried me more. There was only one way to be sure, though, so I focused on the front door and raised my hand to knock as I stopped before it.

"About time you showed up," the man who answered said wryly. He was older, in his sixties, with swept back hair that was mostly gray with some dark brown mixed in. His overly tanned face was clean shaven, and his eyes were hidden behind a pair of large, tinted lenses. A wave of cologne invaded my nose, a smell that made me think of visiting my grandparents.

"Goldie," I said, trying to keep my anger out of my voice. "You said you were going to move your operations out of San Antonio."

"Actually, I said *the Circle* would move their operations." His lips quirked up in a sarcastic smile as he spoke with his Texas drawl that was so at odds with his Miami mobster looks. "C'mon in, son. I made a pitcher, and it should still be nice and cold."

I was about to point out that it was February, and a hot drink would be more preferable. The moment I stepped into his very warm house, however, I decided a cold drink sounded good after all. As we passed the thermostat, I glanced over to see it was set at 85.

"I was under the impression you were taking over the Circle," I said as Harold Goldblatt walked by me to enter the kitchen. He left me in a living room that looked to be transplanted straight from the eighties. Palm frond wallpaper, wicker furniture with lemon yellow cushions, and a couch with a thick plastic cover to keep dust and dirt off the material.

"That was the plan," Goldie called from the kitchen. "You remember those twins from the night at the warehouse?"

He was talking about an incident more than a month earlier. I'd been hired to track someone known as the Magpie, a collector of Nox curiosities. And the person who killed Jack's sister a decade ago when Jennifer Dahlish sent the package containing the coin to him instead of delivering it to a buyer. Jack crashed a meeting of an organization that called themselves the Circle, capturing the Magpie. Goldie promised me to move their operations away from our town if I let him go, and two others had managed to escape while I was fighting a troll to reach Jack.

"I remember two people in hooded jackets. They're twins?"

"They are indeed," Goldie said, walking into the room with two large margarita glasses in his hands. He handed one to me, waving for me to have a seat on the couch as he plopped down in a wicker chair. "Alexandru and Elina Rosu, scions of a very old family that has been a power behind the thrones of Europe for centuries."

"What were they doing in Texas?"

"The Circle isn't just a local organization," Goldie said with a chuckle. "We have existed for hundreds of years, and no doubt will exist for hundreds more. Anywhere money is to be made or power can be guided, we're at work."

I took a drink of the margarita, enjoying the bite of the tequila on my tongue. Few restaurants and bars would make them so strong. A side effect of my condition, as I call my genetic heritage, is that it takes a lot of alcohol to have an effect on me. "Leeches," I summed up. "What do these twins have to do with you being back in town?"

"Never left," Goldie said. "I have my own businesses to attend to, remember." He owned a string of pawn and gold shops across San Antonio, which had recently expanded up the interstate to Austin. Goldie's Cash & Pawn, where WE BUY YOUR GOLD!!! was proudly proclaimed with giant banners. "I intended to leave soon to take up my other work, but two days ago I got a message from New York that the Rosu twins have assumed leadership of the North American operations."

"Should have moved faster," I suggested, shrugging off his obvious disappointment. Goldie had been the man who hired me to track the Magpie, through an intermediary. I'd probably never know for sure, but I felt certain he'd done so with the aim of taking leadership of the Circle for himself.

Goldie waved a hand through the air. "It was my position to take. Everyone knew it. Those Romani brats jumped the line big time."

I lowered the glass from my lips, fighting the urge to squeeze my fist and shatter it. "The twins are Romani?"

Jack might be the one who studied and researched the old myths and legends to learn everything he could about Nox, but I'd gotten an education in a more practical way. By living among them and experiencing their abilities and weaknesses first-hand throughout my life.

Romani were derisively called Gypsies or Travelers, but as was so often the case, the truth was far more complicated. Fearful rumors of centuries past accused the Romani of all manner of magic and curses, but the reality of their powers was even more horrifying when used for evil. A pair of Romani twins would be stronger still, their powers joined and multiplied by the close bonds that formed between those who had shared the womb.

"Don't worry, Walsh, you don't have to worry about confronting them. Alex and Elina are my problem." He grimaced before taking another sip of his drink. "Word has reached me from those who are still loyal, however. The Rosus have sent an assassin to kill me, because they know I can cause problems while their hold on the Circle leadership is still shaky."

"Why should that concern me? I told you to get out of town until I sent word that you could come back."

He laughed, throwing back his head and slapping his knee. "Boy, I like the way you don't pull any punches. Yeah, you did do that, and I didn't listen. You can't expect a man like me to just turn his back on a business he spent most of his life building."

Goldie leaned forward, raising a hand bedecked with gold jewelry to point at me. "What you should worry about, son, is what this assassin will do to our city. If I know the twins, they'll send a heavy hitter, the kind that won't care about collateral damage. I ain't going to go down easy, that's for damn sure. I don't think Dahlish would like what he comes back to if someone doesn't help me stop this guy before he can wreak havoc.

And if you won't help me, I'll just have to bring in a squad of mercenaries who won't hesitate to shoot at any sign of a threat."

That made me stop and consider the situation more carefully. I may not care one way or the other if some internal squabbles caused Goldie's death, but Jack would feel the need to protect the man. Especially if the assassin had the remotest chance of injuring innocent people while pursuing their target.

I drained the last of the margarita in my glass and leaned forward to put it on the glass-topped table. "What kind of assassin are we talking about?"

Goldie smiled, pulling the stub of a half-smoked cigar from his shirt pocket. He stuck it between his teeth, pulled out a flip lighter, and puffed it into life. "Well, there's the rub, son."

* * * * *

After I left Goldie's house, I drove across town to my own. I lived in a small enclave northeast of San Antonio, an area favored by the 'brutes' of the Nox world. The family next to me were minotaurs, and several ogres shared another house farther down the street. No relation to my great-grandfather who was an ogre.

A big reason for choosing this area was the fact that the homes were built with basements. Such an option was rare in most of Texas, because the high clay content of the soil made them a pain in the ass to maintain. The builder, however, had been a member of the Nox community, and he knew that many of his kindred had a predilection for underground spaces.

My basement was accessed through a heavy steel door from my kitchen. The door was painted the same as the normal wooden variety that filled the rest of the house, but if someone without great strength tried to open it, they'd be stymied. The door weighed eighty pounds, and I'd had to spend a week strengthening the door frame to support it before it was installed.

At the bottom of the stairs was another thick steel door sent into an equally thick wall. Most would scoff at my paranoia, but I believed in keeping my tools secure. The last thing I needed was for some bounty to get wind I was coming after them, only to have them break into my house and use my own gear against me.

Through the second door, I stopped to breath in the scent of gun oil and metal. It was a smell that always made me smile, flooding my brain with memories of home. Three walls were covered in shelves and racks, holding the arsenal that I'd built up through my career. One never knew which tool a job might need, so I kept a little of everything.

In the middle of the room was a square of waist-high cabinets. Mostly, they were filled with the ammunition that my tools required, but I also had a variety of other gear that had come in handy on past jobs.

Goldie knew little about the assassin coming after him, beyond the fact that at least one had been sent. He told me about the handful known to have been sent by the Rosu twins for other hits, though, so I had a basic idea of what to expect. The problem was that each of those handful would require a different tool for the most effective deterrent.

I decided to go heavy for this job, and I pulled out a couple of canvas bags from a drawer of the cabinet island. I filled the first with boxes of ammunition, half a dozen knives of varying lengths, and a Kevlar vest. The second bag I filled with the tools I expected to be most useful – a Mossberg pump-action shotgun, a pair of high caliber revolvers, a grenade launcher that could hold ten canisters of varying types, and a .50 caliber machine gun that normally had to be mounted for effective use. Looking at the packed bags, I decided that I had enough stopping power to handle anything that came after Goldie.

I hauled the bulging canvas bags up the stairs, pausing to lock each steel door after I passed through it. In the kitchen, I dropped them on the ground and walked over to the small phone book I kept beside an old rotary phone. It was the same phone my parents had owned, and nothing would convince me to replace it with a newer cordless model.

The cop's number was hastily scrawled on a page near the end of the book. Jack had given it to me once a few years ago, when all three of us had worked a job together. A kobold group that was breaking into bank vaults. I'd been brought in to deal with the pair of trolls they paid for protection, while the cop was there to put the kobolds in cuffs and cart them off to a human prison.

After I dialed the number, I held the phone to my ear and waited through the trilling rings. When the person on the other end answered, I heard police radios in the background, along with three separate officers taking reports at desks near the person I'd called.

"Sergeant Oliver Williams, SAPD."

"It's Nyk Walsh," I said. "Jack said I should call you if things looked like they could get messy."

There was a pause on the other end of the line. "How messy?"

"At least one assassin being sent to San Antonio to kill a man who is highly placed in a worldwide syndicate of power brokers."

"That sounds incredibly messy," Ollie said with a groan. "You're protecting the target? He doesn't sound like a good guy."

"He's not. But he's not the worst, either."

"Fair enough. Call me if you need an extra set of hands, or if you catch this assassin and I need to take them in."

"I do need one thing. Do you remember the woman from the warehouse in January? Can you make sure she's still locked up tight?"

"Cissie Espinosa? The one Jack said was the Magpie?"

"Yeah, her."

There was the tapping sound of fingers on a keyboard for a couple of minutes, and I waited in silence. As my eyes roamed the kitchen, I spotted a cracked floor tile in the corner of the room. Another problem with clay soil is that the house shifted with the changing seasons. I made a mental note to buy a couple of new tiles and some grout.

"She's still there," the cop said eventually. "Walsh, does this have anything to do with the Circle that Jack told me about? He made it sound like a local group, people doing backroom deals that weren't legal but also weren't too evil."

"That's what we thought at the time. It looks like we were wrong."

Ollie groaned again. "Keep me in the loop, okay? If I need to start worrying about some kind of criminal group taking over the city, I'd like to find out about it before they start dropping bodies."

I satisfied him with a vague promise, then hung up the phone. A large part of my job involved working with local, state, and even federal police groups. That didn't mean I thought they were all good guys. Far too often, the bounties I dragged back for court dates and prison sentences had worked as cops in their former lives. Jack vouched for Ollie, though, so that was good enough for me. He was a better judge of character when it came to humans than I ever would be.

The canvas bags slipped perfectly into a couple of long toolboxes that lined the sides of my truck bed. I strapped them in to be sure they wouldn't shift too much during the drive, then got behind the wheel and left the enclave. The minotaur next door was standing outside his door, giving me a wary glance. The Nox could feel something coming.

* * * * *

Goldie was waiting for me at the door when I walked up. I had a canvas bag in each hand, with another bag slung over my back that held a change of clothes and some toiletries. I kept that in the rear seat of my truck at all times, never knowing when I might need to drop everything and head off on a job.

Inside, I dropped the canvas bags and looked around the living room. "You sure you want to wait here? This place is far from secure."

"I ain't leaving my house, son." Goldie's jaw jutted out in defiance. I'd already tried to make him agree to hiding out somewhere easier to defend. "Hiding is the same as admitting I don't have the juice to be the boss," he insisted.

That meant I had to deal with a house that was almost impossible to secure, and a protectee who insisted on going about business as usual. Including visiting his stores and checking in with his employees. The only concession I'd managed to secure was that we'd make those trips in my truck instead of his baby vomit yellow 60s Coup De Ville.

I made a tour of the house, checking each room and gauging where I'd try to enter if I were the one coming in to grab someone. The master bedroom was the obvious place, but it was in a front corner of the house with a window exposed to the street and sidewalk. The better option was to come through the living room, which had a sliding door that opened onto a covered patio in the back yard. The fences were high, and there was enough shrubbery and tree growth to create privacy.

When I unzipped the first canvas bag, pulling out the shotgun to place behind a planter in the corner of the room where it would be easy to reach, Goldie laughed uproariously. "You planning to go to war, son?"

"I'm planning to save your life, old man."

"Hell, just make sure I'm not in the same room when you fire that thing," he said, eying the grenade launcher that I pulled out next. I jacked open the chamber to verify all ten slots were loaded, then bent to slide the weapon under the couch where it would be hidden.

"You just remember to stay behind me if the assassin attacks here." I pulled out one revolver, setting it on the glass-topped coffee table. Then I carried the canvas bag into the kitchen, dropping it behind the round table in the breakfast nook. It wasn't exactly hidden, but it wouldn't be easily seen.

"This ain't exactly the Alamo, Walsh. A big man like you, I'm sure you could take down whoever they send without needing all this firepower."

"What if they send a jotunn? Or a fomorian?" I'd seen both types of Nox at work recently, a battle between them that had been so filled with power that it clouded my mind. Even after Jack explained what had happened, I only had brief memories of portions of the fight.

"The twins are more subtle than that. They only send the big ones if they want a visible demonstration of their power."

"Taking down their biggest rival to leadership of the Circle wouldn't call for that?"

"Only the North American arm of the Circle," Goldie protested. I wasn't sure why that made any difference, but he seemed intent on clarifying the limit of his leadership. "But you make a valid point. Just don't go shooting up my house unless it's necessary."

I snorted at that, restraining the impulse to point out that I wouldn't have to shoot up his house at all if he'd let me take him to a place that was easier to defend. For some reason, I liked the old guy. The clash of his Texas accent and Miami looks amused me, and he seemed more genuine than ninety-nine percent of the people I dealt with. He didn't try to hide the fact that he was involved in shady dealings.

Goldie lifted an arm to look at the chunky gold watch on his wrist. "Time to make the rounds, son. You ready to be my chauffeur?"

I grabbed the second canvas bag, dropped it on the plastic-covered couch, and unzipped it. "If we're leaving the house, you're wearing this."

He looked at the Kevlar vest with raised eyebrows, then patted his expansive gut. "I don't think it'll fit me."

"It'll fit."

He protested a bit more, but finally pulled of his Hawaiian shirt so we could strap the vest on over his undershirt. The straps had a lot of extra material, built for larger frames. It fit me, so I knew it would work for him. As he buttoned his shirt up over the vest, he grumbled over the feel of it. "Damn thing is pinching like crazy. And the neck keeps riding up!"

"Stop messing with it, and you'll get used to it. Would you rather take a bullet to the chest?"

Goldie glared, but he stopped protesting. He grabbed a straw hat from a hook beside the door, shoving it down on his head as he led the way out of the house. He grumbled again as he pulled himself up into my truck. I hadn't thought anyone could make it seem like more of a climb than Jack always did. I was wrong.

I started the engine and pulled away from the house after checking the street for signs of anyone who shouldn't be there. "No smoking," I said, when Goldie pulled out a cigar stub.

"Ain't this America?"

"No, this is my truck. No smoking." I glowered at him until he put the cigar back in his shirt pocket.

"You're lucky I like you, son. Head to my flagship store, the one you and Dahlish visited a while back."

It was a short drive to the strip mall where the store was located. Occupying the anchor location at the end, Goldie's Cash & Pawn was painted blue and yellow, with bright yellow flags flapping in the wind above the windows.

Several patrons were browsing the goods on display. Counters filled three sides of the store, displaying smaller items like jewelry and collectibles. In the middle of the store were larger items, like a fancy smoker and a drum set with the signature of some famous musician scrawled across the largest surface. Lawn mowers and a couple of dirt bikes were arrayed outside the store.

As soon as Goldie exited my truck, he pulled out his cigar and lit it. He shot me a triumphant smile as he blew smoke rings in the air. "Dial down the menace a bit, son. Don't want to scare away the customers." He laughed as he walked toward the store, pulling down on the neck of the vest under his shirt.

A blast of warm air hit us as soon as he pulled the door open. It felt good after the cold of a late February day. Goldie immediately started chatting with a couple of customers, a father and son looking for a gift for the boy's fourteenth birthday. Goldie sized up the teenager and snapped his fingers as a thought hit him. "I know just want you want, young man. Come right this way." He led them over to one of the cases where several rows of sports cards were lined up. The teen gasped when he saw one, with the athlete's signature on the card.

As they haggled over a price for the card, I looked at the coins arrayed nearby. Jack had been entranced by them when we'd entered the store, but I couldn't see why. Gold, silver, nickel... that's all they were when it came down to it. Did it really matter if one was stamped out four days or four centuries ago? The Spanish doubloon at the center of the collection was apparently worth a quarter million dollars, which mystified me.

Motion drew my eye, and I looked up to see a young woman hurrying over to the group near me. She was in her twenties, with a vitality that only the young and innocent possess. The marigold shirt and blue slacks were just as jarring as the first time I saw the uniform.

"Ah, Natali. Help these gentlemen with this card, darlin'. They've talked me into letting it go for eighty bucks, against my better judgement."

"Of course, sir," the young woman said, flashing a radiant smile that she quickly turned on the customers. Her eyes flickered to me, and I saw recognition in them. I was used to that. People my size were uncommon enough that most people who saw me remembered me longer than normal.

"This way, Walsh," Goldie said, waving his cigar for me to follow. He nodded to other customers as we walked toward the rear of the store, where he lifted a section of the counter so that we could reach the door that led to what I assumed to be the storeroom.

Before we got there, an older woman called out for our attention. "You're him, aren't you? Goldie?" She was old enough to be his mother from the look of her wrinkled skin and age-spotted hands. The white pants suit she wore was more elegant than I'd expect to find on someone shopping in that store.

"That's me, sweetheart. Nice to meet ya." Goldie stepped back to the counter, leaning over to reach out his hand to meet hers.

I reacted instantly, reaching out to put a hand on Goldie's arm. What the hell was he doing shaking hands when there was an assassin out there trying to kill him? While this old woman looked as harmless as a kitten, I'd seen far too many people killed by poison needles or electrical conductors.

"Sorry about that," Goldie said around his cigar. "The big guy here is paid to be paranoid." He shrugged and smiled charmingly.

The old woman laughed, but her eyes looked hurt and angry for half a second when she looked at me. "I'm just glad I got to meet you. A real treat."

"That it is," Goldie proclaimed proudly. He winked at the woman, eliciting a giggle, then turned and walked to the door we'd been heading toward.

As I followed him into the back room, I glanced around the rows of shelves. There was more jewelry and collectibles in boxes on those shelves than on display in the store. One cardboard box had "diamond rings" written on it with black marker.

"Have to maintain the illusion of scarcity," Goldie said, seeing the direction of my gaze. "It makes the customers more willing to shell out the big bucks for something. If I put twenty diamonds right on a tray, they'll haggle me down even lower than if there are only two or three."

He led me toward another door, which opened onto a cramped office that barely had room for a desk shoved against the wall. One of the computer monitors was showing a rotating display from the security cameras, while the other had a spreadsheet open.

"My employees maintain a steady log of sales and purchases," he said as he plopped down in the fraying fabric chair. "I pay well, but I also demand a lot of my people. Ten percent profits minimum each month, for one."

He craned his head to look up at me. "This is why I joined the Circle in the first place." He pointed to the screen, filled with words and numbers that bored me even though I didn't focus on them. "They opened up vast avenues to products that I'd never have been able to touch as a regular Joe. You don't want to know how many famous people owe us favors, Walsh. All those signed sports cards? Just the tip of the iceberg. If I wanted, I could have the hottest Hollywood starlet standing out there pressing flesh for fifty bucks a pop. The line would be down the street." He chuckled at the thought, a gloating sound if I'd ever heard one.

As he puffed on his cigar and scrolled through the spreadsheet, I kept my attention on the camera display. There were five cameras inside the store, giving a full view of every inch of the space. Outside, there were three cameras over the door to keep an eye on the goods that were set up in front of the store each day. One of them was tilted higher, giving a limited view of the parking lot.

The old woman was nowhere to be seen, so she must have left the store as soon as we went into the storeroom. Natali was still working with the father and son, and I watched as she crouched down to unlock and open the display case so she could pull out the card the teenager was excitedly pointing at.

Twenty minutes later, Goldie grunted happily as he stood up from the chair. "Business is booming," he said with a smile, smoke drifting from his nostrils. "Now let's go check in on the store on Fred Road."

* * * * *

The afternoon was filled with store visits. Goldie pondered a drive up the interstate to Austin to check on his newest location, but I quashed that right away. We were already too exposed with the store visits, and being on the interstate for over an hour each way opened up a ton of options for an attack.

I also picked up on more of the Circle's operations, thanks to Goldie's inability to sit in silence for more than a few minutes. He loved to hear himself speak, and he'd apparently decided I knew enough that he could open up to me. Aside from dealing in loans and favors, the Circle apparently launched political careers for those who would vote as directed and sponsor any legislation the Circle leadership decided was necessary. It was an organization populated by Nox and human equally, as well. A strange case of shared goals, but then greed and the lust for power transcended all boundaries.

There hadn't been any signs of an assassin, but I refused to let my guard down. A good operator would be watchful, ready to strike at the first sign of a weak spot. Goldie was feeling more relaxed, however, and insisted on going out for a dinner at his favorite steakhouse downtown. A place that was right in the middle of the most popular tourist section of the city.

The streets were packed with people and cars, and navigating there was always a challenge in my truck. The parking garages were too narrow for a dually like mine, so I had to find an open-air lot and take up two spaces. The attendant squawked about it until I gave her the cash to pay for both spots.

Goldie strolled into the restaurant like a king, puffing on the fresh cigar he'd lit as soon as he was out of my truck again. He flirted shamelessly with the young hostess, who seemed to recognize him immediately. There was a city ordinance against smoking in restaurants, but no one batted an eye as we were shown to a private room. Several of the patrons gave him the stink eye, but as soon as they saw me, they turned away quickly. I don't know why. I didn't like the smoke any more than they did.

Two waiters appeared almost as soon as we were seated, one filling glasses with water while the other presented small menus and asked if we'd like to see the wine list.

"Margaritas, son! Bring us two of your finest and keep them coming until I say 'when'."

I looked at the menu, wondering why they bothered printing one when there were only half a dozen selections. Goldie grabbed it from my hand before I finished the list. "You don't want any of that frou-frou nonsense." He was right. I didn't.

When the waiter came back with the margaritas, Goldie ordered two steaks, medium rare, with all the trimmings. I wondered what that meant at a fancy place like this, but since I wasn't the one paying the bill, I kept quiet.

Goldie was unable to do the same. "This is the life, son," he said, leaning back in his chair to puff contentedly at the ceiling. He seemed to draw on the cigar specifically to make the most smoke possible. "You know what I was doing before the Circle, Walsh? I was a shoeshine boy. Hand to God. My father had a stand in a building a couple of blocks from here. We'd show up every morning at the crack of dawn, shine shoes for men who wouldn't deign to notice us on the street, and we were lucky if we made enough each day to pay the bills.

"Then, one day this man sits in the chair. Nicest shoes I'd ever seen in my life. And he says to me 'what kind of life do you want for yourself?'." Goldie laughed, shaking his head. "I told him I wanted to own my own shop. At that age, I thought it would be impossible to dream bigger than that. He sure showed me."

I waited, wondering if he was going to spool out his life story for me, but he was silent as he chomped down on the cigar. A minute later, the waiter arrived with our food. The steak on my plate was at least twenty ounces of prime beef, cut a full inch thick. Small bowls of mashed potatoes, buttery asparagus, and black-eyed peas were set beside it. For a moment, I felt real happiness, presented with a meal that would actually quell my hunger for more than a few minutes.

Fresh margaritas were brought next, and my half empty glass was taken away. They weren't as strong as the concoction that Goldie whipped up at his home, but there was still enough tequila to feel the bite.

I wasted no time unwrapping the utensils so I could cut into the steak. The center was nice and pink, and the meat was so tender I barely had to apply pressure to the knife to slice through it. The first bite was heaven on my tongue.

The door to the kitchen swung open behind me, and I wondered what more they could be bringing. Goldie, seated across from me, glanced up. When he did a double take, his eyes widening in surprise, I didn't hesitate.

I rolled out of my seat, just in time to avoid the large cleaver that sliced into the back of the chair. The man holding it was almost as large as me, easily six and a half feet. His features were lumpish and rough, with a lower jaw that jutted forward. Troll.

As I rolled into a crouch, I reached back to pull the revolver from where I'd holstered it in the small of my back. The weapon looked comically large when most people held it, but it was a more comfortable fit for my hands than most other handguns. A true craftsman always finds the tools that work best for him.

Goldie raised a hand in my direction, stopping me as I started to squeeze the trigger. "Now, boys, cool it. The last thing we need is a confrontation in the middle of all these people. What's your name, son?" He was looking at the troll as he asked the question.

"Mick," was the grunted response.

"Nice to meet you, Mick, even if you were sent here to kill me. I suppose you do know who I am?"

"Goldie," the troll said. I sniffed in derision, surprised he'd managed to keep that thought in his head long enough. His kind weren't known for their brains.

"That's Harold Goldblatt, bucko. Only my friends get to call me Goldie." I wondered if that made every customer a friend, since they all called him that. "You understand that you're just a pawn in a larger game, don't you? The Rosu twins could care less if you kill me or my protector here kills you."

The troll rolled his shoulders in a rough approximation of a shrug. "Pay me to kill."

"Yeah, they paid you. The question is, how much? Because I'll pay you twice as much if you'll go back to New York and kill them instead."

I could have told Goldie to save his breath. Trolls were known for their stubbornness just as much as for their lack of brainpower. Once you convinced one of them to do something, it was almost impossible to talk them out of it.

"No, kill you," the troll said after an awkwardly long pause. He ripped the cleaver from the chair, raising it over his head. My finger pulled on the trigger, and I felt the revolver buck in my hand as it fired.

Blood sprayed out as the slug hit the troll high in the chest. I cursed inwardly, angry with myself for missing the heart that I'd been aiming for. As the troll fell back like a toppled tree, I got to my feet and got a hold on the Kevlar vest under Goldie's garishly colored shirt.

"Let's go," I said, pulling him along. "That won't keep him down for long." Trolls had amazing regenerative powers. It would take a couple of days for that wound to fully heal, but within half an hour he'd be restored enough to come after us again. Had I hit the heart, that would have been the best chance to kill him. Well, aside from chopping off his head. That was guaranteed to stop a troll.

The noise of the gunshot had drawn attention. I saw a waiter appear from the kitchen, stopping in his tracks to gawp at the troll. One of the hostesses was walking quickly toward our private room as I shoved the door open. I ignored her questions and protests that I should stay until the police arrived, and continued dragging Goldie along as I left the restaurant.

"Sorry for the mess, darlin," he said with a cheery wave of his cigar. "Put it on my bill and charge the card on file."

I paused outside the restaurant only long enough to scan the sidewalks. The troll was definitely sent to kill Goldie, but that didn't mean he was alone. When I was satisfied that there was no immediate threat, I pushed him ahead of me and crossed the street. On the opposite sidewalk, I stopped to look back at the restaurant. Several patrons were exiting in a hurry, but none of them were large enough to be the troll.

Goldie hadn't stopped with me, and he was almost at the entrance to the open-air lot when I turned back. I started to jog after him, squinting to see into the darkness that surrounded the cars parked in the lot ahead.

When I saw a flash of white, I thought at first it was just a plastic bag blowing in the breeze. Then it kept moving in Goldie's direction, and my vision adapted to the darkness enough to see it was clothing. A pants suit.

"Goldie! Stop!"

He either didn't hear me or ignored me, turning to the woman with a wide smile when she said his name. He obviously recognized her from earlier at his store, and he didn't see any reason not to greet her as he would any customer.

The woman was reaching out both her hands, and Goldie was raising his own for a handshake. She may have looked like an eighty-year-old woman, but something about her sent my intuition into overdrive. I poured on more speed, running full out.

I managed to grab her wrist at the last second, twisting it and pushing her arm away from Goldie's hand. The moment I touched her skin, I felt tingles run across my hand.

"Careful there, son. She's just being friendly."

"No," I said through gritted teeth. I could feel it now, pulses of heat climbing my arm. My fingertips were already starting to go numb. "She's here to kill you."

The old woman hissed, and in that moment her human mask dropped away to reveal sickly gray flesh covered in pustules. Goldie cried out in astonishment, jumping back as she tried to lunge forward with her other arm out to touch him. I grabbed that wrist, too, twisting both of them until I heard the bones snap. She barely registered the injury, only smiling up at me through rotted black teeth.

"The plague is upon you," she hissed with a laugh.

"Not for long," I said, taking a deep breath. Her eyes widened in shock for a moment, and she looked down as I stuck the barrel of my revolver against her sternum. When I pulled the trigger, I knew there was no way the witch would survive. I dropped my hold on her wrist, shoving her back to fall to the concrete behind a row of newspaper kiosks. With luck, it would be a while before someone found the body there.

"Get in the truck," I said.

Goldie had dropped his cigar, and for the first time I saw a flicker of fear in his eyes as he looked at the woman. It had been smart of the Rosu twins to send the woman. They understood their prey well, knew that he would be vulnerable to such an approach. The man could never resist glad-handing anyone who recognized him on the street.

She was a cuma, a witch that carried the plague to pass along to any that she touched. It had been years since I'd even heard of one, they were so rare these days. Four hundred years ago, you could have found one around any decently sized village. The problem was that I'd touched her skin not once, but twice. Were I almost any other human, I'd have been writhing on the street in agony by now.

I started the truck as soon as we were both in, not even waiting to put on my seat belt before I threw it into drive and stomped down on the gas pedal. As we screeched through the turn onto the street, raising honks of ire from other drivers, I nodded to the phone sitting in the center console. "Call the cop. Speed dial number three."

Goldie didn't argue. He grabbed the phone, pressed the buttons, and I heard dialing as the phone connected to my Bluetooth system.

"Hello?" There was laughter in Ollie's voice. I must have caught him while he was relaxing, maybe enjoying time with his family. I had a flash of resentment, but I shoved it down.

"It's Nyk."

His voice sobered instantly. "What's wrong, Walsh?"

"It just got messy. Very messy."

* * * * *

My head started to feel a little fuzzy as we turned off the interstate. Five more minutes, and we'd be at Goldie's house where I had my best tools. The ones that would take down a troll much easier than the revolver sliding around on the floorboards where I'd dropped it.

"You ain't looking too good, son." Goldie's voice was kindly as he spoke, and he reached out to touch my forehead before I could stop him. "You're burning up."

"I'll be fine," I said. I knew I could make it long enough to stop whoever came after us next. Once Goldie was safe, then I could worry about the sickness that was spreading through my body. I had some general antibiotics in my kit bag that would help ameliorate the effects of the plague the cuma's touch had transmitted.

We turned onto Goldies street, and I pressed the accelerator. Another minute and we'd be inside his home where I'd be surrounded by my tools. Then I'd be ready to hold off an army of trolls, if necessary.

I was slowing to turn into the driveway when a large SUV shot out of the driveway across the street. It had been screened by a row of tall pencil cypress trees, so that I had only seconds to brace for the impact as it rammed into the side of my truck.

Glass shattered beside me as the door crumpled under the force of the collision. If not for the money I'd spent strengthening the frame, I would have had a shattered arm and leg at the very least. Instead, I was only bounced in my seat, my head cracking against the top of the door frame.

The SUV's tires were squealing as it continued pushing my truck, and we bounced as the tires skidded over the pavement until we slammed into a car parked at the curb. When the SUV stopped pushing, Goldie and I were trapped in the truck with both doors blocked.

I looked over to find him slumped in his seat, the belt holding him up. There was blood trickling out from under his hat where the side of his head had impacted against some part of the truck. His chest was rising and falling, so I knew he was just out of it for a while.

Getting my seat belt off proved to be a struggle. The latch refused to release no matter how much I pushed on it. I tried to lean over and open the glove box for the knife I kept there, but the belt was holding me too tightly. I looked through the spiderweb cracks in the windshield as another SUV screeched to a stop. The doors opened, and two large trolls climbed out.

I recognized the weapons in their hands immediately, because I had one of them sitting in the house only fifty feet away. The first projectile ejected with a *ka-thunk* sound, and I watched the cannister arc through the air. It hit my windshield and bounced off as white smoke began to pour out of the grenade.

Another grenade hit the windshield, the glass continuing to hold up under the assault. I knew that wouldn't last if they moved on to explosive grenades instead of trying to smoke us out. I grabbed the seat belt in both hands and strained against it with all of my strength. It took longer than I expected with the ravaging disease beginning to weaken me, but soon I heard the first sound of the material ripping. With a last effort, the seatbelt split apart raggedly.

With freedom restored, I bent and felt around for my revolver. There were still four rounds left. It was too dark to see it, and I realized belatedly that the streetlights on this block were unnaturally dark. That should have been a warning that someone had laid an ambush, if I'd been thinking straight.

Glass shattered nearby, and I looked to my left to see a boot only slightly smaller than my own slam against the windshield of the SUV again. The safety glass broke free, falling onto the crumpled hood. The man who stared at me from behind the wheel looked very much like Mick at the restaurant, and I wondered if an entire family of trolls had hired themselves out to the Rosu twins. I stopped wondering quickly, as the troll raised a shotgun.

I ducked down as far as I could as the weapon fired. A hollow thump sounded above me, and I felt the small beanbag round drop onto my back. The gun fired again, and this time the windshield couldn't hold up to the abuse. The cracks were too extensive to give it the strength required, and it broke open.

"Now shoot," the troll trapped in the smashed SUV shouted.

At the same moment, my fingers found the revolver. I wrapped my hand around the grip, sitting up to face the three attackers. The first smoke grenade entered the truck, but I ignored it as I focused on my target. The right tool for the job.

One of the trolls standing in the street was thrown backward as my bullet took him down. I hit dead center on his forehead, blowing what little brains he possessed onto the pavement behind him. The two other trolls howled with rage, and both fired their weapons.

Another smoke grenade entered the cab of my truck, and I started to cough and tear up under the assault. The beanbag round fired from my left barely missed me, flying past the tip of my nose to hit Goldie's shoulder. He grunted, his eyes flying open at the pain of the projectile.

"What's going on?" he asked, his eyes darting around.

I didn't take the time to answer, swinging the revolver around to point at the troll in the SUV. I pulled the trigger as soon as the sight was centered on one of his eyes. His head bounced back against the seat before flopping forward. Two down.

The last troll shouted with rage, and I saw him pulling out canisters to reload his launcher. I had a strong feeling these wouldn't be smoke grenades.

"We need to move," I said to Goldie as I reached over to release his seat belt.

"Where the hell are we going to move to?" he demanded, looking at the roof of the wrecked car blocking his door.

I pulled him forward, then shoved him between the gap in the front seats until he fell onto the rear bench seat. I had to strain, but I was able to reach the almost hidden loop that let me pull the seat's back down to expose the sliding door I'd constructed for situations like this. "Through there," I said, pushing Goldie.

He muscled the door aside, and I winced as the metal squealed when it scraped together. The hole exposed was just big enough for him to squeeze through, large belly and all. His legs were disappearing into the covered bed of the truck when I heard the thump of the grenade launcher firing again.

I whirled to grab the projectile from where it landed on the seat Goldie had occupied a minute earlier. In my head, I was doing a count, reaching seven as I tossed the grenade through the windshield backhanded. It landed in the street, and the troll just had time for the shock to register on his face before it exploded.

Shrapnel pinged against the vehicles, and several small pieces cut open my skin as they blew in my direction. The last of the trolls was thrown off his feet, landing ten feet away in the road. It would be enough to slow him, but anything short of a direct hit wasn't going to kill him.

"Come on," Goldie yelled, his hand waving for me to follow him.

I twisted around and hung through the gap between the front seats, stretching out to get a hand on the sliding door. "Stay there until I come back for you." He looked at me in confusion as I slid the door closed. I lifted the seat back until it clicked into place to hide the panel.

I'd had the bed of the truck constructed to protect any important cargo, such as bounties that pissed me off and I didn't want to ride in the truck with. It would be strong enough to keep Goldie safe in case there were more attackers.

My mind at ease, I turned and holstered the revolver at my back before I started to climb through the windshield. I had to shove it a few times, creating a hole large enough for my body. Shards of glass pressed against my palms as I crawled out onto the hood of the truck, but none of them broke skin.

I dropped down to the pavement, rolling my head to loosen my tense muscles and pop my neck. When I looked back at my truck, I felt my anger growing. My baby was a disaster, and it was going to take weeks to repair the damage the trolls had done to her. Both front tires were flat, making it look like she was almost kneeling in the pain.

The crunch of gravel was the only warning before the troll landed on my back. His fist swung over my shoulder, embedding a three-inch blade in my pectoral. He started to twist the knife, but I reached up to grab his arm. I was no longer angry.

I was furious.

Bones snapped under the force of my grip as I pulled the troll over my shoulder. He landed on the hood of my truck, howling with pain as his back cracked in a way that didn't sound pleasant. Blood covered his face and torso, ragged tears in his skin that were stitching together even in the few seconds I looked at them.

The troll snarled at me as I kept my grip on his forearm. I turned to the side, wrapping my other arm under his chin and around his neck. As I squeezed, his snarl faded into a grimace of pain.

"How many?" I asked.

The troll tried to shake his head, a refusal to answer. My hand squeezed again, and both forearm bones shattered under my grip. There are times when I stop trying to moderate how much of my strength I use.

"How many?"

"Five. Only five."

I stared into the troll's frightened eyes, my lips set in a frown that promised dire things. I decided I could probably accept his answer as truth, but as my father always said: *trust, but verify.* I pulled, gritting my teeth as I strained with all of my might. The troll howled in protest, and then screeched in pain as the tendons and muscles began to rip. I kept pulling until the arm tore free from his body, tossing it away like the trash that it was.

"How many?"

"Five! I swear! Only five!"

His eyes were filled with pleading now, not a trace of defiance or deception to be seen. I nodded, feeling relieved to know this was almost done. My other arm began to squeeze, and the troll's face went bright red. He tried to beg for mercy, but I wasn't listening.

Once that was done, I dropped the head to the pavement and went around to check the other two. Both were dead, but I put another bullet into their hearts to make sure. Then I pulled the troll out from behind the wheel of the SUV so that I could reach in and shift it into neutral. I pushed it back from my truck, all the way back to the opposite curb.

The door was so mangled I'd never be able to open it. I was able to reach in and pick up my cell phone from where it still rested in the center console, though.

"Walsh? Is that you?"

"Yeah. Was the guy who attacked us still at the restaurant?"

"Yes. We had a unit a block away, so they got there in less than a minute when the staff called it in. They have your guy in cuffs. He won't say much, though."

"Trolls are too stupid to think up explanations," I said, breathing a sigh of relief that he was off the board.

"The body, though..."

Too soon. "Yeah?"

"Our people combed that entire parking lot, and we didn't see anything. There were some dark spots that could be blood, but that was all."

The cuma never should have survived a shot to the chest. My revolver would have put a hole in her back the size of a dinner plate. But at least I didn't have to worry about her coming after Goldie again. Not for a long time. Even if she did manage to live, she'd be recuperating for months. The witches were cowardly, too, preferring to strike from the shadows whenever possible. Without someone like the trolls to back her up, she'd run.

"Do me a favor. Make sure the troll is locked up at least for the night. I'll deal with it tomorrow."

"Come down to the station and make a statement, Walsh. Then we can slap charges on him."

I scoffed at that, smiling wryly as I ended the call. Maybe Goldie would go down and put in the complaint about the troll attacking him, but I didn't think he'd be any more eager than I was to do so. As I looked at the wreckage of my truck, I looked forward to when the creature was released.

A wave of disconnected numbness swept through me, and I clutched the door handle as my knees went weak. I'd put too much energy into the fight against the trolls, and that let the plague spread faster.

Goldie bolted out of the truck bed as soon as I keyed in my code to unlock the cover. "Where are they?" he asked, looking around wildly.

"They're dead," I said, lowering myself to sit on the raised bumper. "You're safe for now."

Sirens sounded in the distance, and I wondered what had taken so long. Then I looked at the phone in my hand, and I realized it had been less than ten minutes since the SUV rammed into us.

"How the hell are we going to explain this?" Goldie asked, his face turned in the direction of the sirens. We could see flashing lights in the night now, no more than a half dozen blocks away.

"I'll take care of that. You were never here." I looked at him until he nodded, then jerked my head for him to leave.

"Walsh..."

"Never here, Goldie. I'll come back for my tools tomorrow or the next day. Don't touch them."

He shook his head, smiling as he reached out for my hand. "I owe you, son. I owe you big."

"You can repay me by making sure those Romani don't send anymore assassins to Jack's city."

Goldie's mouth compressed to a hard line. "I promise you that won't happen. I guess it's time for me to confront my problems head on, instead of trying to approach it from the side. No choice now." He looked toward the carnage in the street, no doubt shocked that so many of them had been sent to ensure his death.

The sirens were closer now, and there wasn't much time before the police cars turned onto the street. And hopefully an ambulance or two. A few doses of antibiotics would knock out this plague thanks to my strong constitution, unless I waited much longer to have it treated. My head was starting to feel woozy, and I was seeing two streets when I looked up again. Goldie was gone.

As the first police car appeared, screeching through the turn, I thought about what Jack would say right now. He'd probably make some stupid joke about how the arm I'd torn off could grow into a new troll. But I think he'd also say that I'd done good.

And when it comes down to it, that's the best a man can hope for.

About the Author

After more than 20 years of working IT support for a nation-wide bank, I decided it was finally time to start putting my imagination to the page. Creating stories and new worlds has been second nature for me since I was a kid, and I've wanted to be a writer since high school.

If you'd like to keep up to date on my projects, visit my web-site at www.timrangnow.com. You can sign up for my monthly newsletter there and get access to exclusive short stories and early peeks at upcoming books.

Dahlish Series

Lost Souls

Memory and Sorrow

Dark Deception

Fateful Knights

Awakenings

Other Books By Tim Rangnow

Guild Series
Vagabond

Indomitable

Waterloo

Resolute

Rim Jumper
Prime Example

Viridian Skies

Pirate's Nest

www.ingramcontent.com/pod-product-compliance
Lightning Source LLC
Chambersburg PA
CBHW031946240626
47153CB00003B/873